Wanderers in the Void

Their memories of the time before the Cataclysm had faded or had never been. They hunted their prey on the barren land, companions who had fled the stifling confines of Shelter Town.

Then they met Eve.

It was the end of their long journey —and the beginning of a mystery they would risk their lives to unravel . . .

THE JUDGMENT OF EVE

THE JUDGMENT OF EVE

Edgar Pangborn

A DELL BOOK

To M.C.P

Published by
DELL PUBLISHING CO., INC.
750 Third Avenue
New York, New York 10017
Copyright © 1966 by Edgar Pangborn
Dell ® TM 681510, Dell Publishing Co., Inc.

Reprinted by arrangement with
Simon and Schuster, Inc.
New York, N.Y.

The author wishes to express his thanks to
Random House, Inc., for permission to use an
excerpt from the translation of *Grimm's Fairy
Tales* by Margaret Hunt, revised by James
Stern, copyright 1944 by Pantheon Books, Inc.

First Dell Printing—December, 1967
Printed in U.S.A.

PART ONE

May Night

1. A Loneliness of Women

The young woman blew out all the candles but one and set a fresh log on the fire. Her mother had fallen asleep after rambling on a while about East Redfield and the days when that town existed, a stop on the bus line from New York to Boston; when there were bus lines and you took them for granted; when East Redfield had a population of more than six thousand. Eve could not visualize so great a number of human beings, even scattered over a large area like the town place a mile away.

Its rooftops had been in sight until a few years ago, when expanding tree growth hid them from Eve's favorite lookout in the upper pasture. Now nothing of the town could be seen even in winter, for most of the trees in the new forest were pines, dense and vigorous and full of music under the winds.

Six thousand people, all different? Different names, different kinds of work to do, habits, personal quirks, degrees of goodness, badness, intelligence? Perfectly impossible, but of course true. The books as well as Mama said it. But it remained beyond reach of imagination. The brain was compelled to accept; the heart could not avoid confusion, unwillingness, dismay.

The city of Redfield, Mama said, had been growing out in all directions back in the 1960s and '70s. *Before I was born—oh, naturally there had to be such a time, but . . .* They called our town a metropolitan bedroom, said Mama—so many living in East Redfield, commuting to their work. You know, twelve miles was no obstacle at all in the age of the automobile.

Eve could picture buses moving on the roads, since the dulled body of one was serving as a section of their brush fence and had done so ever since she could remember. It provided a ratproof shelter for storing grain. The word "metropolitan" was a little blurred for Eve by lack of any need for it, but she had not wanted to ask an explanation; she could look in the dictionary tomorrow by daylight. Mama was obviously tired, having been up and around too

much, feeling her way through the rooms, fumbling at
housework she ought not to attempt; still, it made her
more restless to be steered away from it, and Eve found
it painful at any time to argue with her. Mama could
distinguish strongly illuminated shapes, she claimed, and
she liked to think that her fingers were getting more clever
all the time.

Those who used to tell the legend of the Judgment of
Eve in a civilization much later than hers, and occasionally write it down, usually allow that the girl was about
twenty-eight at the time of her most important decision;
the written accounts generally differ about many other
points. Assume she was twenty-eight, and for this account
at least assume her to be a goodhearted, affectionate
wench, with a sweetness about her like the color of summer mornings (the color they had before we grew old,
the color they seem to have had occasionally even in that
century of smog and fatigue, the so-called twentieth).

Eve was lonely and oppressed by the knowledge that
her mother, at sixty-five could hardly have much longer
to live. Eve supposed that after this inevitable death she
would take to the road. Impossible to imagine staying
here alone with Caleb, unless he begot a child on her. A
child of his could resemble him; Mama said so. Merely to
think of the nightmare of the begetting, supposing the
poor monster was capable of it at all, was a horror past
bearing. That had to be ruled out. Human nature forbade
it.

In the midstream of her talk about East Redfield, set-
tling a blanket close about bony shoulders and crinkled
neck, Alma Newman had wandered into that shallow
sleep. She looked, to Eve, not so much defenseless as remote. Rouse her, and Alma Newman's self might have to
swim up through some incomprehensible abyss within her
and peer through the nearly sightless eyes without much
true recognition. And yet, wide awake, the small lady belonged very much in the present world.

Living, for Eve, was waiting; time, a continuation of
the many thousand days and nights. The body matured;
sadness grew like a more leisured night, the heart unwilling to spell out the plain reasons. Sometimes Eve thought
she understood what she waited for—theoretical names and
appearances—but could not guess whether desire would
continue if suddenly her waiting ended. It puzzled her to

find that the waiting was endurable at all, seeing what latent fires she knew to be smoldering within.

She had been living too long with visions made out of the air of nothing. The books were drained. Well, not that; they can't be. Her brain was at fault, incapable of winning more from them, because what she called boredom had become at twenty-eight a torment hardly relieved even by sleep.

She heard Caleb lurch up from his pallet by the kitchen door and pad from window to window. He would probably come in here and look out toward the old bus, the disappearing gravel road. He could not see in that direction from the kitchen.

The long complex of house, woodshed and barn stood at a right angle to the road. The buildings, put up about two hundred years before, followed a New England design developed for snugness and practicality in a time when (Mama said) the winters must have been more severe. A lean-to sheepfold stood against the barn; it could be shut securely at night. The chickens had the run of the barn itself now used for little except their needs and the storage of as much hay as Caleb was able to harvest with a scythe, cure, and fetch in on his back. (Eve had to sharpen the scythe for him, but then he could swing it with fair skill and seemed to enjoy the exertion.) This last March the five ewes had dropped only three lambs, not including a deformed one unable to live. But, as in other years, the hay never seemed to be more than just barely enough to get them through the winter months.

Eve watched her mother to learn whether Caleb's noises were bothering her. Mama looked calm, the stern white head drooping against the padded wing of her chair. Defenseless, remote, but very much Mama, Mrs. Alma Newman, still the ruler of this isolated fragment of space and eternity.

Caleb did shamble meekly into the fireplace room and halt his ugly mass at the east window. His rancid and earthy smell was too familiar for Eve to be annoyed by it. He was always uneasy in this room, cramping his ponderous shoulders to make himself seem small. He peered through the glass into the dark—sweaty, loud-breathing, male at least in shape and crude as a half-modeled lump of mud, great soggy hands at his eyes to shut away the glow of the fire and the candle. The moon had not risen.

Caleb's sunken yellow eyes had undoubtedly noticed everything in the room—the state of the fire and the woodbox, her mother's sleep, her own inadvertently careless sprawl that might have let him glimpse her thighs as Mama said she mustn't do. Caleb was, probably, harmless —well behaved all these years anyway, remembering an old lesson. But, Mama said, there was no point in disturbing the poor beast.

He left the window, uneasy but not making his dim speechlike noises. The whitened old scars on his right cheek, left arm and right leg showed starkly as he swung around to lumber back into the kitchen.

Mama's blacksnake whip had ripped his flesh open in three strokes—left, right, left. Long ago. Eve could watch clearly in memory the violence of her mother's arm, the set coldness of her mother's face, calm as if she had been preparing the action for a long time in advance—she had —and the leaping of Caleb's blood at the cuts. Eve recalled not too plainly what had gone before, only that the Monster Boy had grown excited, followed her about from room to room whimpering and making curious displays. It happened right here where they were sitting now. Scared by Caleb's following, she had ducked and run for the doorway just as her mother stepped out of shadow on the other side of the fireplace. Then a whine of leather through the air—it had once been Great-grandfather's buggy whip, Mama said—three dry explosions of the punishment and Caleb's howls.

You'd hardly imagine it now to look at the old lady.

Mrs. Newman had been in difficulties later, trying to explain the incident to Eve without creating false terrors. Eve could not in maturity recall just what sort of ideas about Caleb had followed her through the rest of childhood. An understanding that Caleb couldn't quite be treated as a playmate, but was only a useful and potentially dangerous pet, something to be controlled by kindness if possible, if not, then by a measured cruelty. (Mrs. Newman had considered equipping the child herself with a whip but decided against it, reasoning that ownership and use of it would do Eve more harm than Caleb ever could. In or out of the restraints and opportunities of civilization, you take certain calculated risks.)

Caleb himself did not lose the lesson. Must never touch.

Left, right, left—never, never and never.

As for the scars, Caleb probably gave them no thought, yet Eve knew he did occasionally slip into the shadowed front hall to examine his image in the mirror. It did not apparently excite him. His feeling might not go beyond a dull wonder as he pawed at the glass. Perhaps he knew the mirror self was not quite living. He surely hadn't any way of guessing that he was hideous.

Not opening her eyes nor moving her head from the wing of the chair, Mama asked, "What did he want?"

"A look from the east window. Acted as if he'd heard some noise. I didn't. I thought you were asleep."

"I believe I was for a moment. Everything locked up?"

"Yes, Mama. I saw to the locks an hour ago."

"I hope he didn't hear a panther. It's such a tiresome uproar when they come close. Is it still April, dear? I'm ashamed, the way I lose track. Those lovely calendars you used to make! Now that I can't see them I do lose track."

"It's the first week of May, Mama."

"Well, I was close. It's that time of year, the buds and the sap and trouble in the heart. The cat creatures make a great fret in the spring. That's sex. With us it's that and all the other human wishfulness along with it—don't think I don't remember. The snow's all gone?"

"Yes. There wasn't much. Didn't you tell me there used not to be panthers in this part of the country?" Eve sensed that her mother was in a mood for talk, and the subject of panthers was likely to prove entertaining. Eve herself had glimpsed the animals once or twice, vanishing smoky-tawny, the shape of terror but hardly the reality, for the books as well as Mama called them timid things— timid with man, at least.

"That's right. They were found only out West, where they were called pumas or mountain lions. In older times, though, maybe the time this house was built, they were around here. They were called catamounts by the colonials, and later on too. No harm in them for human beings— oh, once in a great while, maybe. They keep down the deer. When I was a girl we used to hear rumors about a few of them still to be found in the East—in the Adirondacks, the Laurentians. Most people didn't believe the stories. Panthers turned up again soon enough after the troubles, after hunters and guns and crowded towns and cars and planes were gone. It didn't take any of the wild things very long to notice how peaceful the earth was. Did I doze off just now, Eve?"

"A little. Two or three minutes. You were tired."

"I suppose. I had a dream, one I've had before. I may have told you about it. I dreamed of hearing people not far outside the house, searching, maybe for us. Have I told you?"

"No, Mama."

"My nice liar. Probably bored you with it a dozen times." Eve never knew how far it was right to go on deceiving Mama. "If I'm growing forgetful at least I'm somewhat aware of it. That particular dream is almost pleasant. You see, I have the idea the searchers are people I know, or might have known. There's something wrong or at cross purposes between me and them, but I have the feeling I'll be able to set it right, and I'm going out to greet them, when I wake. Sometimes I imagine—this isn't a dream, dear, but just fancy and partly memory—I imagine quiet houses with their doors unlocked. A boy and girl talking together a little way down the street, hidden by a thick maple, and none of their words quite coming through to me." Eve wondered whether her mother might be consciously trying to rouse up the aches of loneliness. Why? Mama didn't do things without a reason. "She laughs—teasing him, you know. There's all the spring softness—some evening in May. The talking ends and I know they're kissing good night. . . . We must try the road this summer, Eve, as soon as the weather settles and the snow—oh, you said the snow . . . well, dear, I know, I've said this before but I mean it: this summer we must get out of our rut, take to the road in spite of the risks—we must and we will. . . . It's odd I should imagine my little love scene that way. When I was young and kissing boys good night we'd be sitting out in a parked car, likely. More petting and wrestling than just kissing. Then when the boy left it would be with a racket of six or eight cylinders."

"Cylinders?"

"Part of an automobile engine. Don't ask me to explain how they worked. All I ever heard about mechanics went out the other ear. I used to drive competently, but I was helpless if anything went wrong. . . . I thought I heard wolves last night."

"Yes, they were chasing something, sounded more than a mile away, the other side of Wake Hill, I thought."

"You were seven the first year I heard them. It was the same year Caleb came to us. He seemed to be about ten or twelve, as near as I could guess. I'd never heard them before, you know, anywhere, but I knew . . . You've had a look at the brush fence lately? It's such a worrisome time when the lambs are young?"

"I went over it today. Seems to be all right."

They heard the door from the kitchen into the woodshed open and close. That would be Caleb going out to make sure all was well in the barn and sheepfold. A thick rope hung from a loft window of the barn. When the doors were locked and bolted Caleb could go outdoors and return by that route. The loft window was too high for a panther's leap; no large animal would try the rope, except Caleb.

The old woman brooded. About Eve, as usual, who had been not quite three years old when Arnold died, who had seen no human nature since then except her mother's and her own. Not including Caleb. Aloud Alma Newman said, "A wolf is only a big wild dog. The wolf in human nature is a thing you've never seen—well, a commonplace way of speaking, I suppose you've encountered it in the books. Just a way of saying human nature has latent cruelty and violence in among the other qualities. . . . Can't remember your father at all?"

"I try to sometimes, Mama. Nothing comes except things I know you've told me. I don't find a real memory of my own."

"He was a good man. I've tried to give you the truth about him without letting my memory magnify too much. His world considered him impractical—same world that had already gone out on a limb and was cleverly sawing away at the butt end with its eyes shut. He wanted to keep this place a farm, in a time when that kind of farming was crowded out of existence by earth-mining operations that had made farming a dull, mammoth business, partly destructive, no longer a way of living. He farmed this patch of ground, and tried to write a few books, and scraped together what money he could from odd jobs— professional typing and what not. Couldn't get his books published, and a lot of his farming ventures went wrong too, from lack of strength, equipment, money, experience. A miserable life for him. He was called a crank and a failure—one can see why. But he was my crank and I'm still proud of him. I worked part time too when I could. We got enough to eat. We never felt licked, those years. . . . I must have told you how the old bus got stuck out there?"

"I wouldn't mind hearing more about that."

Arnold had that tactfulness too. Alma Newman sighed in her blindness, blaming herself for weakness and fear. Certainly they should have taken to the road five or ten years ago, when she could still see. It had been so easy to go on thinking that some others would come—and now Eve had grown to be twenty-eight! "Well, the old hack was carrying ten or a dozen East Redfield people who'd picked up some silly rumor about a train being made up at Addison for the West. A train! Why, even at that time the old railroad probably didn't have a sound tie anywhere from Addison to the main line; but people believe what they want to believe and no cure's been found for it yet. Our gravel road did run all the way to Addison, twenty miles, a short cut from East Redfield. I remember a lot of people persisted in the notion that things were somehow better out West. It could have been an old tribal itch, because in earlier days the drive of expansion had been in that direction. The lemmings run down to the ocean where once there was solid land. This was a full two years after the one-day war, remember, the second year of the sicknesses. The red plague was everywhere in the East, or so we understood from what little news came through. With electric power gone, the few battery radios didn't last long. No new batteries. Silence. Silence and rumor, so the ancient fears and fancies and superstitions rose like scum on a pool gone stagnant. The oceans were large again—do you understand that?"

"I think so."

By the time some were screaming that Russia was responsible for the plagues we could hardly be certain Russia still existed. A name for something that perhaps never had been real, on the other side of a world that recovered great size. Well . . . Well, I heard the noise of the bus and saw it come toiling up in a mess of black fumes. Heaven knows what they had for fuel. I didn't go outside. Arnold was dying. He had come out of our room in the delirium of the red-plague fever and fallen—over there, if I'm pointing in the right direction, near the front door. I couldn't lift him. You and I were both sick with the

same thing, and you less than three years old. I wrapped
blankets around him, he was shivering so. When I heard
the bus I went to the window, stood behind the curtains to
watch. They stalled, right in front of the house. East Redfield already had word that we were down with the red
plague, so I knew those people would never come near us
—and what could they have done? I just watched. Oh, I
thought of going down to them—I suppose I did."

"They . . . wouldn't?"

"It was not surprising, Eve. Two days before, some
people we had thought of as friends had stopped by and
almost run away when they learned Arnold was sick.
Still, I don't know that there was actually more callousness,
cowardice in those days than in earlier times. I don't think
there was. The twentieth had no more meanness than
other centuries. People had merely lost some of their
handiest cover-ups for meanness, and so were more open
about it. Anyway, as I said, no treatment for the red plague
was known, so what could they have done? I watched.
Heard enough to explain what they were trying to do, the
imaginary train at Addison and all that. It was *funny*, Eve.
Sick as we were, and Arnold dying, I had to laugh at them.
I was probably lightheaded with my own fever, not thinking plainly. The bus motor choked and went dead. The
driver got it started again, but momentum had helped them
up that hill in the spring mud, and without it they were
helpless. No maintenance for two years—the road was a
terror. I watched the bus dig itself in, that fool driver
spinning the wheels. The hind end sank like a circus
elephant sitting down. That's why it has that tilt even now.
Frost heaving over the years hasn't altered it much. There
it stayed."

"We've had good use of it."

If I could see her smile! I think she did just then. Alma
Newman tried to win the image of Eve's face as it must
be now, two years since her eyes had been able to see it.
Wasn't it more like three years? But she could not picture changes in it, or would not. In her last remembered
glimpse, it had been a brightness clarifying out of a blur,
coming down out of the glow of a candle to kiss her
good night. "Yes, we have. Of course the rust will get
to it after a while. I remember two women with babies in
that group. I forget their names, though I did know them
well enough at the time. And there was an old man mak-

ing himself impossible, shaking his fist at the driver and
yattering about things he had to do before the train left,
for the legal protection of his property. I knew him too.
It was Clint Shellabarger, the druggist, never did have a
grain of sense. Legal protection!" Eve's eyes, she remembered, were like Arnold's, a smoky blue-green, under a
broad forehead and hair of reddish gold. Her upper lip was
soft and expressive, a gentle and sensual delight.

Alma Newman wondered sometimes whether an artist
would find the girl beautiful. Other men certainly would
(but there were no men). Alma herself—long ago, before marrying Arnold Newman—had posed for a lively
traditional artist who called his charming portrait inadequate; but the old boy had been a transplanted Florentine
and might have been lying, charmingly, just to carry on a
cinquecento tradition in the century of deodorants, pop art,
Billy Graham and singing commercials. She went on, remembering: "The others tried to quiet down old Shellabarger. There was some whispering and glancing up at our
windows, but I knew there'd be no contact. I really didn't
want any, Eve. There was nothing they could have done
for Arnold if they'd had the courage. They went on afoot,
and Shellabarger was still waving his arms and bleating
about legal this and that, and I felt that a great deal was
passing away from me, a great deal more than just a bunch
of . . . lemmings. I can't imagine there was really any
train at Addison. I'd driven over there a little while before
the war—that far back—and even then there was grass
growing between the ties."

"Those people were following nothing but a rumor?"

"Probably. There wasn't too much else you could do
in those days—follow rumors, or stay home with a loaded
rifle. I think a whole month passed after that bus stalled
before I was able to walk down to East Redfield. You
were still weak; I carried you most of the way. I had
managed to dig a grave. It had to be shallow. I carried
flagstones from our front path. You were talking pretty
fluently at going on three, but I had trouble making you
understand your father wouldn't be returning. You'd
whimper for him when you woke up and search the
house. Well, down there in East Redfield, no one at all.
Only a few dead people in the houses. There was a filling
station. I wonder if you remember that by any chance?"

"No, I don't think so."

"Someone had taken an ax to one of the pumps. The ax was still lying nearby, a good one. I brought it back with us. It's one of those Caleb still uses. . . . Maybe we should go down to the village some time soon, Eve—I mean, the place where it was. I don't think we went last year, did we?"

"Well, no," the girl's voice said, "nor the year before."

"What! We skipped two years?"

"It was difficult, Mama—everything so grown up, long stretches where pine needles covered up and hid the road. And in some places where the old gravel did show there was new growth pushing right up through it. I guess I could still find the road this year, but it wouldn't be too easy."

"I see. I've been losing touch, I know. We must have Caleb cut some kind of path. Of course down in the village we can find the main roads. I can remember watching men and terrific machines working on those, Eve. Bulldozers, rollers, back-hoes, mixers—I don't know what all. They have deep layers of crushed rock under the concrete—couldn't possibly have broken up in twenty-five years. Put some more wood on the fire, dear. I'm cold."

Alma Newman listened hungrily to the sounds, trying to imagine, behind the gray barricade of the cataracts, the grace and easy motions of the girl. Girl? A woman, a tall woman of firm flesh and deep tender breasts that might never give suck. She felt the comfort of a stronger warmth reaching her bones. "Eve, I don't think you like it much when I talk about the old time."

"It's not that, Mama. But sometimes I sort of lose you."

"Well, it was a flawed world. Honesty was out of fashion. The religions were falling apart like old rotting logs, but all the same people still had to have one consoling falsehood after another if it killed them. It did kill them. Rembrandt and Beethoven may have been killed at the same time—I wish I knew. There must be libraries and museums standing, here and there. It was easy for us sophisticates to say we were all guilty, as if that kind of breast-beating served some purpose. Not even true, in a rational way of looking at it. I, Alma Bradford Newman, dropped no bombs. 'We are all guilty'—no, that was never much more than a whine, a way of dodging responsibility by seeming to accept it. Help me up to bed, Eve. I think I might sleep."

The sustaining pressure of Eve's arm—even that stirred in Alma Newman a sense of guilt. The old woman thought: *I am draining her vigor. We must take to the road, not just think about it and cringe away while she too grows old.* She tried to make her step seem confident on the stairs. There were eight risers, then the platform making a right-angle turn, and two more of his steps. *I lost count! I lost count!* But Eve's arm turned her with casual care; the panic passed. Undressing and getting into bed, she accepted Eve's help with less than usual of her attempted independence. "You've locked up?"

"Downstairs? Yes."

"I meant here."

"Not yet. After all, Caleb never comes upstairs."

"Lock it anyway. He can move so quietly. And it's getting toward full moon. Isn't it? Didn't you say it was getting near the full?"

"Well, yes."

"And, dear, I hate to fuss, but don't forget about the shade when you undress."

"I won't, Mama. Please stop worrying. I think poor Caleb is completely—what was the old word, the scientific one?—completely conditioned against anything like that. I know—the full moon, he gets a little wild, but I can't imagine him coming after me. He justs works it off somehow, and all his senses are dull."

"I know. You're right. Sometimes I worry just like an old woman." When she felt Eve's kiss the light that her eyes imagined remained quite unchanged, although Eve must be bending down between her and the candle. So doubtless the light was an illusion of the blind. "Good night, Eve."

How can I leave her, so completely alone? Drifting toward sleep, she thought fretfully of Caleb. She should have gelded him when he first came, she supposed—a boy not very big; she could have done it then, when she saw what he was. He never did grow a real beard, only a few mean hairs that needed to be trimmed—a job she had to leave to the girl now. Was Eve doing it, or letting the ugly hairs grow? Didn't matter. She clenched the blanket and forced her fingers to relax. Kill him? Surely not—surely he was more a protection than a danger. If it ever came to a test, he might fight to defend Eve, like a good dog. The hard part was the thought of leaving her alone, Caleb or no Caleb. And that could happen any time—next year, next week, tonight. Still fretting, Alma Newman found sleep.

Caleb felt his way through the barn, touching a few objects to guide himself but hardly needing to, for his yellow eyes saw fairly well in the dark. He liked to move his horny bare feet silently. There was muscularvisceral pleasure in that sense of stealthy quiet, like the pleasure of peering out of a snug shelter unobserved. Noises bothered him, for they often meant he must stir himself and there was always the chance they meant danger. Or they could mean something was required of him by the two beings who ruled his existence, the only sources of guidance and objects of devotion.

About thirty years old, Caleb had no memory of beginnings. No people but the two women existed for him, and his mind was too weak at making comparisons to understand that they belonged to the same breed as himself. For him yesterday blended into last year; what happened two or ten or twenty years ago could have happened this morning. He did not specifically remember the whipping, but it had effectively broken any relation between woman-shape and sex. The sight of Eve now made no connection with the yeasty sexual hungers that occasionally rose up in him, and (as Alma Newman supposed but could not know for certain) he could not have touched Eve's body any more readily than he would have laid his thick hands on the top of the stove.

The small candle of his mind groped smokily on from moment to moment. He felt; he learned a few simple things now and then. Stimulated by the speech-sounds of his deities, he was able to connect meanings with a number of simple words, though he could not reproduce the words and knew he could not. To his own ears his gargling noises were never quite satisfying, and he had no impulse to imitate the delicate sweet sounds the women made. A normally endowed chimpanzee could probably have outsmarted him most of the time, and at thirty he was growing old.

He stole respectfully past the chickens' roosting place, his nostrils twitching in dislike at the strong odor of their bodies and ammoniac droppings. He had once been seriously whipped for killing and eating one of those, and again for killing a sheep. The law was then firm in his mind, and he was no longer bothered by the originally confusing fact that some other creatures could be killed. When he managed to hit a rat with a flung stone the women were delighted with him. And he learned that he might kill, if he could, any rabbit or woodchuck raiding the garden. They did so Themselves, with the bow and arrows he must not touch, sometimes with the guns that were even more strictly forbidden to him. But when he got one of those he must always give it up, and They would prepare it for eating and give him a share. Contradictorily enough, they wouldn't eat rats, but recoiled from them.

Once he had strangled a wildcat that had trapped itself in the woodshed and attacked him. For that They petted and praised and soothed him, washing and bandaging the wounds. Then they stripped off the hide and did queer things with it, and now Mama sometimes wore it around her shoulders, and it smelled of her with all the cat odor gone.

The loft window from which the rope hung looked to him slightly paler than the blackness of the barn, making him feel that this could be an important night. He did not precisely recall the moonrise of the night before, but sensed that tonight might show an even more splendid whiteness in a clear sky. It would be a night to go outside and roll in the grass.

He took off the trousers he had been taught to wear during the daytime and whenever he was in the house. (Eve fixed them for him nowadays—Mama used to—a new pair miraculously appearing every so often, with speech-sounds that meant he must give up the old ones to be washed.) He took surprisingly good care of them, folding them now rather skillfully and laying them on the edge of a haymow in the dark. So far as he knew, it was not against the law to be naked when alone at night.

He would go outside presently and wait for the white light, but it wasn't there yet. He strolled into the sheepfold and petted those friends awhile, fondling them, mumbling his noises, occasionally clasping one with indecisive mounting motions. Familiar with his smell and touch, they hardly waked to notice him. He drifted away, restless. Later, on the grass under the big white light, he would roll about and rub his dull loins against the earth until a flabby explosion of nerves relieved him.

He climbed the ladder to the loft window and sat above the earth waiting for the moon.

He had forgotten the dim and distant sounds that had troubled him earlier and sent him to the window in the fireplace room. At his perch now in the loft window he heard them again, and rumbled in his throat. Unfamiliar always meant unwelcome. If the unfamiliar happened to be a sound, Caleb's neck and spine tingled with the raised back hair of ancient ancestors.

This sound was remotely akin to the blatting of a small flock of sheep a long way off. Caleb felt the similarity with no articulate comparison and dismissed it. He knew where his own sheep were, and so far as he was concerned those were the only sheep in the universe. He had never encountered sheep in the woods, therefore they didn't exist there.

The night was full of noises. He knew the sounds of owl and wildcat, the high metallic ring of a fox's bark, a panther's wail, the squeal of a caught rabbit, shrilling of cricket and tree toad and rasp of katydid. Having no names for anything, nor even any images for the creatures such as owl or tree toad or whippoorwill that he had never seen, Caleb was still familiar enough with the multitudinous music of spring night to understand that what he heard now, to his left and a good distance down the hill, was strange and new, therefore not right.

It made him think, just faintly, of the noises he could make in his own throat. It seemed to be drawing nearer, though very slowly, through the lower woods. He growled and shinnied down the rope and circled the house.

No light was showing except the one candle They always left burning upstairs through the night. He stepped carefully, alert, prowling in defense of his own, dangerous. He had once driven off an exploring bear with rocks and the pitchfork and the courage of utter ignorance.

He clambered ape-fashion from the hood of the old bus to its roof and squatted there disturbed, listening, growling. A sense of unknowable power approaching spoiled any pleasure he might have taken in the full moon's rising for the month of May.

In this account of the Judgment of Eve, Caleb is reduced (almost in the manner of the twentieth century) to a plain mental defective. Because that's what he was. If he shows up poorly as a monster or Cyclops or bewitched prince, as twenty-fifth-century raconteurs evidently liked to have him, he is even less satisfactory as a twenty-sixth-century significant symbol. Just the poor halfwit who did the chores, including woodcutting, and rolled in the grass.

The old woman slept, unaware in blindness of the May moon. Eve slept, after a time, her face turned away from the whitening sky because the spring moon necessarily deepened her pain.

2. The Candle

Kenneth Bellamy observed the moon's rising through a break in the corridor of pines. He wished his companions would pause to enjoy it. Surely neither Ethan nor Claudius lacked an eye for the beautiful. He remembered his father's explanation: the moon was a sort of planet, smaller than the earth and somehow dead, reflecting the light of the sun; also the old man's comments on the sin of pride in those people of the latter-day Sodom and Gomorrah who believed God would actually permit men in their manifest wickedness and whoredom to be sent to the moon. Amen.

To Bellamy's vision and uncertain footsteps the overgrown gravel road had not ceased to exist, but he wondered how he managed to go on believing in it. Ethan up front was proceeding softly as smoke. Maybe he could see in the dark; Bellamy could almost believe it of his bearlike friend. Sending back occasional warnings of obstacles to avoid, Ethan's voice was cool as that of a man in middle age, but in spite of his poise and his fierce red beard, Ethan was very young and still inclined to accept Bellamy as a sort of volunteer big brother.

Bellamy relied for guidance mainly on his acute hearing. It told him Claudius too was climbing the slope with hardly a stumble. For a leader, wasn't old Claudius spending considerable time in the rear? Bellamy chided himself: a Shelter Town kind of thought, and unjust. In a situation like this the man with the youngest and sharpest senses goes in front: Ethan, no competition.

All this hill-climbing for the dubious glimpse of a lighted window maybe two miles away! Uphill through a mess of brush and pines, gravel you could hardly find, shin-breaking rocks, and all black as a witch's box. And what if it was real witchcraft? Why should a lamp or candle be shining up there? Claudius and Ethan had claimed they saw it. It could have been an early star.

So far their journey, when Claudius was not searching side trails, had been along the great road between shadows of wilderness. No settlements, only spots of desolation like the ruined village in the valley where they could at least have spent the night under cover. A disintegrating graveyard, but it had roofs and doors. Now they would sleep in the open again, with all its terrors.

Spirits of the village's dead, he supposed, might have been angry at their trespass, if there were such things as spirits—he felt he should be openminded about that. And he must do Claudius justice in his thoughts. The little man would surely take the front place whenever their trio needed his qualities for a spearhead. Tonight, for instance, if they did find human beings up there—if the light wasn't a supernatural, some Willie Wispo or Jack of the Lanterns trying to lure them over a cliff—then no doubt Claudius would speak for them and show them what to do.

Claudius claimed he held no belief in the supernatural, and Bellamy respected the strange older man's opinions —more, at least, then he respected those of anyone else. Still, didn't it stand to reason that there must have been something wrong with the way children were educated back in the time when Claudius was growing up? Not that Shelter Town was necessarily doing any better, but the old-time people were responsible for the disaster, weren't they? Who else, if you couldn't believe in a vengeful God? Bellamy's father had. Bellamy's father had said —in his last moments too, repeating it clearly when he was dying—that God was altogether displeased with the human race. As in the time of the Flood.

In many ways, the old man hadn't been entirely sensible in his last years there at Shelter Town. He went forth and preached to the birds, no one else present to listen except a bewildered small boy who had to kneel at the correct moments and repeat difficult large speeches. Bellamy's mother had been staying with friends in New York

City at the time of the one-day war, and the old man often explained how this was a judgment on her sinfulness; the boy never quite discovered what the sinfulness was, and later on it seemed strange to him that so many million others had to be annihilated in the same blast of punishment. Had they all committed the same sin, and weren't there any innocent people among all the millions? Would a just, merciful, omnipotent God demolish the innocent with the guilty? The old man wouldn't lie, would he?

Kenneth Bellamy couldn't quite remember his mother. At thirty he found it possible, even easy, to assume that his father was mistaken about one or two things, maybe.

For all his own life he would carry inside him a dim recollection of a world that was. A glow rather than a memory. An awareness, mainly inarticulate, of a light so blurred by intervening mist that no effort would reveal its true shape, or quality, or source. He had been five years old on the day the war began and ended, and he recalled nothing of the day itself. The nearest of the physicists' toys had fallen more than three hundred miles from his New Hampshire home town—fallen somewhere south of New York City, which ceased to exist. Then for Kenneth the move to Boston with his father, the years of collapse and the plagues, the move to what became Shelter Town. No memory of the day of war, but he could examine a number of luminous images from the time behind that day, his first five years. He recalled the tactile and visual sensations, and the smells, of riding in what must have been the front seat of an automobile, yet he could not bring back with any clearness what the machine looked like from the outside—merely a vast red nothing-much that dissolved into the semblance of the many others he had been aware of on the road.

Some versions of the legend make Kenneth Bellamy an improbable blend of Columbus, Leonardo da Vinci and St. Francis of Assisi. He did explore, but not in the geographical sense; he does seem to have invented or reinvented a method of paper-making, but it's not known that he ever painted a picture in his life, or wanted to. As for preaching to the birds, Ken was perfectly willing to let them figure it out for themselves. This version prefers to see him as confused and human—a good joe, very bright, with a number of weaknesses that didn't prevent him from having a nice disposition and being hell on the women.

He was also cripplingly nearsighted, a serious misfortune in the world he was obliged to inhabit. After his seventh year, the final year of the plagues, no one was available at Shelter Town who was competent to diagnose the condition, and there was no industry left that could have made lenses for him even if the technique itself had not been lost.

He could be fairly sure of the expression of a human face five feet away. The moonrise gave him no brilliant disk but a diffuse white splendor interwoven with grey of cloud and uncertainty of stars. He had been taught reading at Shelter Town, and he virtually exhausted the books in that small, unhappy settlement, his hunger unappeased. There had been a lot of careful thought about survival tools, seeds, technical manuals, weapons; no one apparently had done much about storing books that were just books.

It was a small refuge almost on the coast, south of Boston, with an artificial underground cavern that was never needed. Other shelters must have survived the time of troubles—maybe out West. At Shelter Town no contact was ever made with them. Memories perished and certain habits of thought. Other habits survived and flourished, since the raw material of superstition will never give out.

Bellamy's myopia lent a look of dreaminess to the big smoke-gray eyes of his friendly, classically regular face. Sometimes a tension abruptly appeared, which only meant that he was trying to make out something indistinct, but the change was startling. Women found that exciting, taken along with his handsomeness, tallness, strength, his skill at turning an erotic compliment, his genuine interest in feminine thoughts and feelings. To Bellamy women were people, a cause of success with them which, by the way, can't be faked. He had not lacked for undercover love at Shelter Town, though it had to survive in the chilly shadow of a puritanical mood, increasingly dominant in that place, which the town fathers usually called liberalism. He had recently been offered a stern choice: get married or devote his services to a stud system known to the Shelter Town administrators as the Fatherhood of the State.

The State was an area of ten square miles, once a suburban subdivision plus a bit of farmland. Modern housing, sandy and stony ground, that cavern, a strip of beach, population of intellectuals, dairy farmers and clam diggers, about four hundred and not getting bigger all the time. Many of the women were sterile; one heard the death penalty proposed (but not yet enforced) for contraception; the sternest advocates of this remedy were compelled to admit that dead people are poor breeders. As a "controlled bachelor, junior grade," Bellamy would have been allowed no contact with his children (he rather liked kids) and would have had to live mainly on wholesome thoughts and tomato juice.

Three weeks ago Claudius had arrived from nowhere with the spring rains, dressed in sturdy shabbiness, carrying a light bow and small arrows—a wonder that he could manage even those with his damaged left arm—a fine hunting knife, a pair of binoculars. He talked of starting a new settlement. Examined by the Shelter Town administrators, he said that in several years of exploring what used to be New England and the other eastern states he had happened on several isolated families, some of whom had agreed to join him if he found a suitable location and enough others to form a community. Asked how many such families there were, he grew thoughtful, more observant of his questioners, and replied: Oh, a few, a dozen or so—his settlement would have to start small.

Uh, your settlement? said the town fathers. (Poker-faced among the spectators of the inquisition, Kenneth Bellamy and Ethan Nye were saying to Claudius Gardiner a silent, joyous *Yes.*) Uh-huh, my settlement, said Claudius, and smiled.

The Shelter Town authorities then explained to him in a perfectly nice way that his idea had been excellent or at least understandable (though just a mite *ambitious,* perhaps?) while he was still unaware of the existence of Shelter Town. Now, of course, having come to a successful, enlightened, God-fearing community already well established, it was his duty to bring those poor isolated families this way, at once. An escort would be provided, with ample supplies and so on. By the way, he must have written down directions for finding these people? Be awful careless if he hadn't. Why, no, said Claudius—sorry, all in my head. Well, said the fathers, then you may act as our guide. Taking some time for reflection, but not much, the little black-haired monkey of a man hitched his

binocular case—the black was silvering but he might still
have been on the warm side of fifty, with that radiant,
somewhat bitter, somewhat wicked smile on the unscarred
side of his face—and said, well, sorry, he guessed he'd be
perpendicularly God-damned if he'd do that.

The town fathers decided to overlook the blasphemy,
blaming it on an immoral education acquired in the old
time, though a minority did feel that three or possibly four
hours in the stocks might be good for him in his hardness
of heart and conscience. They were all wounded and bewildered, however, and so felt it necessary to pop Claudius
into jail.

Searching him, they discovered no directions, only his
bow and arrows, binoculars, knife, a fine straight *razor*
like the one Bellamy had inherited from his father, and a
volume entitled *Leaves of Grass*. Shelter Town's useful
one-volume encyclopedia explained that Walt Whitman
was a nineteenth-century poet. The book was, as they expected, dreadful, full of subversive, incomprehensible,
improper language. It was entrusted to the jailer, who
fortunately couldn't read, along with Claudius' other pos-
sessions, until it could be formally burned and some satisfactory method of dealing with Claudius Gardiner himself could be worked out—banishment perhaps. Thus
Claudius had no difficulty in picking up his things after
Kenneth Bellamy and Ethan Nye gave him a lift by belting
the jailer over the head with a length of cordwood—soft
maple, not hard.

In spite of his ruined left arm Claudius could doubtless
have broken out of the makeshift jail by himself. It was
merely one of the suburban dwellings not at the moment
in use, built c. 1965 and rapidly falling apart. Claudius was
warmly grateful, though, for the intervention of his new
friends. Bellamy and Nye set out with him on the great
lonely road through a chilly April night, into the larger
world of which he knew a little and they nothing.

After three weeks Bellamy's enthusiasm was partly
eroded. He felt inadequate. He still admired Claudius,
or supposed he did, but found it hard to like him outright.
There was chronic bitterness in Claudius, incomprehensible
humor; the man talked too much about that lost world
which to Bellamy and Nye must always remain a mystery.
Claudius used many unknown words. He could be appall-
ingly direct, or so it seemed to a man brought up in Shelter

Town, where circumlocution about sex and religion was felt to be somehow the basis of morality.

And Bellamy had not quite understood how harsh a handicap his defective vision would be, until he came with it into places where every step meant potential danger. Panther, bear, wild dog and rattlesnake were not much more than rumor at Shelter Town. Claudius took their near presence for granted and wouldn't let you forget it. On the broad road that survived from old time Bellamy felt reasonably competent, but Claudius had repeatedly taken them away from it to trace out some blind secondary route, recording it on a map that existed only in his mind. This hillside in the night was for Bellamy a small hell even after the moon's rising. And back on the big road in full daylight he had often been distressed by his inability to see a normal distance into the green sea that everywhere flowed up against the concrete barrier.

That sea was not to be forever thwarted by any such obstacle. In many places dense Virginia creeper and other vines for which Bellamy knew no name flung themselves clear across the huge ribbon and found anchorage on the other side. Try to lift them and you learned with what insolent power the tiny red fingers grasped the road surface, in league with time. Their vegetable patience insisted: Maybe not now, or now, but after a while . . .

Ethan sniffed the air, admitted his uneasiness to himself, and said: "Stop! Hold up and listen a minute."

Ahead of them there was certainly a clear space. White waves of cloud were barred across by only a few sparse lines of branches. Ethan Nye felt against his face the whimsical push of a trifling breeze. It carried the hint of a stale smell. Nothing too bad, something like human sweat and dirt. He wondered whether Ken would be scared by it. Once he had supposed Ken could do anything, go anywhere and never be frightened—and this was not the only occasion when Ethan had been puzzled to learn how hero worship doesn't last. But Ken was a good guy, an old friend and a good guy.

The smell drifted from somewhere straight ahead, maybe from the same place where he had heard or imagined a low-pitched noise like a growl. Catamount or just possibly bear—but Ethan had been a wilderness hunter for Shelter Town since he was fourteen, one of the lonely, competent men whom Shelter Town people admired, used, feared, cherished and never listened to, and he knew this smell wasn't right for either animal. He glanced behind him, locating the spots of pallor that were the faces of his friends. He said, "I'm going ahead slow. You stay back a little. It's a clearing, a big one, I think, and something— you hear it too?"

"Thought I did," Claudius said. "Dog?"

"It's not dog smell. Watchdog would've barked, or rushed us by this time, wouldn't you think?"

"Likely."

"You keep, say, ten paces behind me. Something jumps me I don't want to go tumbling back onto your cold iron."

"Fair enough."

Bellamy had not spoken, but the moon's face came free of a mask of cloud, and Ethan could see the tall man clearly, even to the faint network around his eyes and the shining of the weak eyes themselves. A good guy, but maybe not much to him? Muscle, yes, but fight? Hadn't been proved. The old boy had sure pissed up a storm when they took him out of the library and put him to work at the town dairy farm, but you couldn't be certain whether he was missing the books or hating the cows. And it had been Ethan who faced the necessity of taking a chunk of wood to the jailer Pete Sawyer. Ken would've stood there arguing until old Pete had time to gather his wits and squawk.

Claudius too was more visible in the strengthening light, and Ethan wished once again that he could find a word or two for the unfamiliar state of mind the little ugly man had brought about in him. Good clear words sometimes dispelled confusion or at least suggested ways out of it. He felt loyalty for Claudius—but that didn't say enough. Love, but that said too much. It was like a friendship but stronger, like lust but weaker, like fear, uncertainty, wonder, recognition all known in the same instant. It seemed to him that you might know everything your brain could take in about Claudius, and he would still be a stranger. And maybe, just maybe, his feeling was something like the worship he had once given to Big Joe Nye, the boss hunter of Shelter Town who was generally credited with being Ethan's father and who had been killed—*Damn, six years ago, wasn't it?*—by a pack of wild dogs. Ethan considered that mental connection curi-ous, and probably some quirky foolishness on his part.

Claudius never looked the least bit like Big Joe Nye.

(Big Joe, huge and taciturn, had gone out alone after deer—he never should have gone alone—and might have carried a bottle with him, a fault he had; he said they ought to call it a God-damn virtue because it held down his wenching. Tumbled over a bank apparently and broke his leg. The dogs found him in the night, if they were dogs; could have been wolves. When searchers located the ruin there was enough to tell the story—rags, a big boot, tracks spattered over crimson snow. It was really the only occasion when wilderness—magnificent, indifferent, totally heartless—had reminded Shelter Town of the truth of its dominance, in fact rubbed Shelter Town's nose in it. Since nothing more of that sort had happened in six years, Shelter Town's nose was about ready to be rubbed again.)

Loyalty was a good word even if it didn't explain enough. Ethan had not said to himself that he would lay down his life for the crippled, possibly mad stranger Claudius. But if at this moment some night terror had rushed them he would have flung himself between it and Claudius, not thinking, or thinking with his muscles.

One can dismiss the Paul Bunyan image that twenty-fifth-century storytellers made of Ethan Nye. He never did strangle a bear, but he could crack walnuts in his elbow. He was a splendid friend and a bad redheaded enemy, and what he did in the events of the legend will be recorded. What more? You should have spinach?

Ethan stole ahead to the edge of the woods. A house stood beyond a high-piled fence of brush. Some faint illumination from an upper window touched the leaves of a white oak. Then Ethan was out from under the trees, in the clearing, on bare gravel. The moonlight shone at maximum power, and Ethan saw the Midnight Star beginning the arc of one of its strange rapid passages across the northern quarter of the sky to the northeast. A hundred feet ahead of him, about forty feet from the snug low house, loomed a tall oblong slightly tilted, with a metallic appearance except where a wild grapevine looped over it. They had passed the ancient wreckage of such things on the big road. Vehicles, Claudius said, and of course he knew. From the top of this thing a crouching shape observed them, a shape resembling nothing but a man.

Bellamy had come up too close behind. "What's that big square thing over at the right?"

"A house. Keep back a little." What help was a companion with no strength in his eyes?

Nothing was to be gained by waiting. Ethan stepped ahead in the full flood of moonlight—nobody to fool with. He liked letting his red hair and beard grow out in shaggy disorder because Big Joe had always done that. Ethan's broad face displayed the proud, somnolent good nature of a lion and of a man.

(It did hurt him that back in Shelter Town they never had called him Big Ethan. A long time now since Big Joe died, and it wouldn't have cost the schmucks anything, but naturally you could hardly ask for it. Nicknames were important in Shelter Town, marks of distinction, a handy way of acknowledging a man's salient qualities and so allowing him to stand out from the group. He had other grievances against the place. It was a sanctified bore, and the bouncingest women were usually off limits for one reason or another in spite of all the earnest talk about increasing the population. Since leaving Shelter Town Ethan had not spent much time on memories of it. His devotion to Claudius was an experience so new and puzzling, so seeming-improbable even to himself, that it made him wish to walk carefully in the wilderness of his thoughts.)

The man-shape lurched up to man-height. The growl became a mumbling chatter, pathetic. Now why, Ethan wondered, should he be thinking of it so? What ailed him? Going soft? The thing was human but in a miserable fashion, naked and gibbering. If it threatened them seriously he would not shrink from destroying it. He watched its blobby hands thrusting out toward them. That could be a threat or an appeal.

He walked forward with easy slowness, halving the distance before he stopped. Bellamy and Claudius followed. They were near him in the powerful white light, too near in spite of his warning. Ethan liked elbowroom. His hand lay on his knife hilt, and he hoped there would be no need of it. A good hunter, Ethan had never harmed anything human nor desired to.

The man-thing was tall, gross, almost without a waist.

Claudius stepped past Ethan, who had unhappily almost known he would. Ethan said, "Watch yourself, Boss. Whatever he is, he's nerved up."

"I think it's all right." And there he was, out in front with his hands empty.

Out here the gravel reached to what must have been the original borders of the road, blurred only here and there by encroaching weeds. The house and its attached barn were to Ethan's eyes handsomer than anything in Shelter Town. This crude, naked man-animal could scarcely be the owner of all that. There was the hint of a civilized light upstairs.

Bellamy muttered, "That a man up there?"

'Something like. Let the Boss handle it."

The voice of Claudius tried a gentle probing: "Who are you? We won't hurt you. Come down. Talk to us."

The brute moved suddenly and swiftly from his roost and came toward them in a rush that looked ugly, but stopped short ten feet away from Claudius before Ethan had time to get in front of him. There it stood trembling, dim-faced, perhaps relaxing out of suspicion and wrath.

Bellamy had placed himself where he should, on Claudius' other side, and echoed a few of the soothing words: "We won't hurt you."

Clear and close in the white light, the naked man's face now seemed to Ethan not downright hideous, just flat and dull. A thick nose, flabby lips, skin coarse but except for a curious scar not marked by any lines of thought or experience. Nothing was excessively out of true, and nothing quite right either.

Children in Shelter Town as well as elsewhere sometimes discover the clay of a mudbank and mess about with it making lumpy animals, people, heads. Without skill or much motive to improve, they usually grow quickly bored with the role of God and walk away, perhaps leaving a clod with sorry eye holes to stare at eternity till the next rain.

The scar on the naked fellow's cheek was much like the grayed whipping scar Flint Sawyer earned some years ago when he was caught with Administrator Borden's young wife, trying to implement the Fatherhood of the State according to his own notions. They shoved Flint in the stocks, the Public Corrector was instructed to give him one lash on the cheek, fourteen on the back, and Flint was (unofficially) heard to snarl that it was almost worth it. Gossip claimed—correctly, as Ethan happened to know—that Mistress Borden's lashes were administered in private and not on the face—that is, a week later they were still sore, but he couldn't see that they cramped her style 'too much, the darling. Ethan stared at the moonlit house, warmed by this and other recollections of Amanda Borden. His senses were focused as much as necessary on the lumpish man, who now seemed harmless, defenseless—in fact, the poor fool was crying. There must be real people in that house. Women.

"Who are you?" Claudius asked. "Can you talk to us?"

"Uh . . . uh . . . uh . . ."

"What do people call you?"

"Cay . . . cay . . ."

"Don't be afraid of us, Cay."

Bellamy said, "Don't cry, man! We won't hurt you." Claudius was a little startled at a new richness in Bellamy's voice. Always resonant, a singer's voice, it acquired from Bellamy's present feelings, whatever they were, an exaggerated quality of tenderness and warmth. Bellamy probably didn't know it and couldn't help it. He surely had no reason to put on an act for this vague monster.

The thing stumbled forward squirming its hind quarters like a cringing dog, patting the ground, groveling, and knelt, not weeping now but slobbering and smiling, at Bellamy's feet.

A laugh might have been safe but Claudius Gardiner suppressed it: the noise could distress or even enrage Caliban. After all he was not immune to resentment in his darkness:

> This island's mine, by Sycorax my mother,
> Which thou tak'st from me.

"Ken," said Claudius, "it looks as if you were elected God. See if you can get him to show us in. Must be some gate arrangement in that brush fence, unless visitors are expected to climb over the Redfield Traction Company."

"Maybe," said Ethan, "no visitors allowed."

"You could be so right." Claudius noticed that Bellamy was bewildered and disgusted. The idiot did smell; he squatted at Bellamy's feet worshiping or waiting for guidance or just existing. "It's like this, Ken: you're the tall, important-looking character with the big voice, while Eth and I are the satellites, the slobs that only a mother could love. Eth is too big and I'm too ugly. It makes you top brass."

"Brass?"

Shall I never remember that language itself nearly died?
"I'm sorry—old-fashioned expression, slang. The point
is, this man is an idiot, what we used to call a mental defective. Haven't such things turned up among the Shelter
Town children?"

"There's something in the law," Ethan said. "Mr. Borden explained it to my age group once. Something about
if a person is born mental he has to be isolated."

"O Mental, how art thou translated! Well, clearly
that's not the law here. What did they mean by 'isolated'?"

"Like put out in the woods."

"I see. Jet age to Neolithic by way of euphemism."

Frowning in the moonlight at the unknown words, Bellamy groped at it: "Men like this get born without a
brain?"

"With a weak one. This fellow might have as much
sense as a four-year-old child. Not enough so that he
could teach himself or grow any better."

"Horrible. But why does the poor thing choose me? I
didn't understand what you said about that."

"Your tallness. Your voice. Maybe this crazy moonlight does something to your face that he likes. Anyhow
you're stuck with it. He evidently understands a few
words but can't speak. Ask him slowly, the way I did,
what people call him."

"What do they call you? Do they call you Cay?" And
Bellamy was quite good at it, Claudius noticed. Natural-
born social worker or something. He sighed, reproving
himself. It would be stupid as well as unkind to under-
estimate Bellamy. The man had all sorts of latent qualities that only needed a chance to grow.

"Cay . . . luh . . . luh . . . luh . . ."

Ethan laughed. "Eth, watch those noises," Claudius
said. No harm had been done. The idiot gave Ethan only
a casual glance and returned to his worship, slobbering
and patting Bellamy's moccasins.

"Will you take us to the house, Cay-luh?"

"Make it a command, Ken. Questions bother him. Nobody asks them of an idiot."

"Take us—over there—to the house, Cay-luh."

The idiot giggled and with encouraging backward
glances led them in a scramble over the hood of the bus,

up a path where old flagstones alternated with bare trod-
den places, and past the front door of the farmhouse without a glance at it. "In olden days," said Claudius, purposely making his voice loud and yet casual, hoping to
lessen the alarm of anyone within who might hear, "New
Englanders out in the country seldom used the front door
except for a few special glad celebrations like weddings and
funerals. Later came the age of the door-to-door salesman
—that is, the age of iron. And yet in New England, by
God, even the Knights of the Fuller Brush were compelled to do their homage 'round back, otherwise no dice."

"Boss," said Ethan, "what in the hell are you talking
about?" Under his breath he added, "I saw a small foot-
print back there—moccasin print, in the soft earth just
off the path."

"A child's?"

"No, but much smaller than the idiot's. Maybe a woman."

So brace for a storm. Still, Claudius thought, it was
part of the search, and maybe the most vital part, for himself as well as for the boys, who were naturally woman-
starved. *Leader material, Mr. Gardiner? Damn, I never
claimed it. Just happened.* His crippled left arm ached,
the ghost of the arm in torment for a part of the past that
could never be renewed. He was going to have one of his
sick times presently, and no dodging it. Ken and Ethan
hadn't seen that yet. *Damn the thing, can't it hold off a
little?* "Where the devil's he taking us now?"

The idiot had gone past the side door too. He was at the
barn, where a rope dangled from a loft window, and he
was trying to shove the rope into Bellamy's hands.

That homely side door and its diminutive porch had spoken of the deep past to Claudius, born fifty-one years before in the state of Maine. His family had moved to
Boston when he was eight. In spite of all that happened
later—wandering, much study, a few years of what is
called fame, the death of a civilization—countless images
of childhood remained unharmed in the amber of memory. A hayfield at the edge of hemlock woods gathered
into itself the heaviness of midsummer afternoon. The
whine of Hampton's sawmill two miles away was no in-
trusion but an acid pleasure in the hush. Evening, and the
blended voices of robin and wood thrush and the white-
throated sparrow. They still sang in that part of the world,
more happily no doubt with the sawmill long quiet. The

side porch of Claudius' childhood had never been without the rocking chair where Aunt Wanda liked to sit for her sewing, a needle-tongued nineteenth-century antique. There would be garden tools and often Pop's boots, because he was sensible about not tracking up the kitchen and getting scolded for it.

By the side door of this moonlit farmhouse in the here and now, no boots, no rocker, no Aunt Wanda heaven knows; nevertheless a pail had been turned over to drain. He saw a mop and a broom, a rather odd-looking broom, standing like obedient waiting soldiers.

The ground-floor windows of this house were protected by thick wooden bars—old two-by-fours—nailed against the frames. Behind the partly obscured glass Claudius was aware of white curtains. In this world some women still believed in white curtains at the windows. With bars.

"He seems to want us to climb this rope," Bellamy was saying. In the sweet musical voice there might be a hint of proprietorship. Bellamy the big kid. Maybe on second thought he wasn't altogether displeased at being elected God.

"Wouldn't hold me," Ethan said. "I must outweigh Buster by fifty pounds at least."

And Ethan had picked up "Buster" from Claudius, a label most unsuited to the dignity of Shelter Town thinking. "Not for me either," said Claudius, "with my glass arm. Come on back. We'll have to knock anyway like civilized people."

By daylight the side door would look aged and dingy, in need of the kind of paint men could no longer manufacture. Just an old door. The broom interested Claudius. Its stick was machine-rounded, therefore more than twenty-five years old, but the straw had been tied on with heavy string (the string itself probably valuable beyond price) and the straw was some native makeshift, oat straw perhaps, certainly nothing like the tropical broomweed that old-time housewives used to take for granted.

Under the moon the door hinted at feminine modesty, primness. Claudius felt, in his overdeveloped right arm, a hesitation, as if he were about to grasp something too vulnerable, a bird too young for flight, a child's doll house. Ethan was too damned big. *What am I doing here? What right . . .*

"What's the matter, Boss?"

"Nothing, Eth. I'll be all right in a minute."

"You look—"

"Never mind it. Stand by. Let me be. Don't say anything." His intensely strong right hand found the wooden pillar supporting the porch roof. He accepted the necessary pain as the flesh of his fingers bruised itself between wood and bone.

He had never found any way to prepare for it in spite of the few minutes' advance warning. First the dizziness, the strangled impulse to fight something; then the reliving, his mind conscious in protest all the while but unable to halt or change or soften any of it. No begging off. Nothing to do but take it like a victim of migraine or an epileptic and get it over with.

In his sick fancy the earth twitched under him as if to dislodge a burden. Then he must hear the landslide roar of collapse, must reel and drop at the unbelievable impact of stone, gasp in the blinding dust, the pressure of darkness. Time saved itself, not confused. In the dark each heartbeat shook him, a blow from within, but he could count them, he could understand that eternity was a simple matter of, say, fifty-odd pulsations. A nothing—you just sweated it out and stuck around.

After that, the rest need not be a reliving but only a rational memory, too vivid but sane, eyes open, the here and now reforming itself in light and color, while in memory his right arm was toiling against the block of stone that covered his left—and winning at last (not quite time yet for the pain), winning quite impossibly, since no human being had any right to be able to overturn such a weight as that. But winning anyway, so that he could remember looking down along the rope of bleeding tissue, crushed and worthless, a skinned worm, and saying as if there could still be a place for sanity and argument, "But I am a violinist."

Scholars will have already noticed that this version of the legend relies most heavily on the *Notes on the Life of Claudius Gardiner, by Himself*. There is no other recourse, if one is trying to achieve the dignity of history. No other surviving document has more than a fanciful bearing on the story, but this one, infuriatingly oblique and incomplete as it may be—well, the style and state of mind are authentic twentieth century. Bryce-Leong and other authorities attest the genuineness of the twentieth-century notepaper. What can we do except admit that somehow this scrappy fragment of autobiography did survive the centuries of confusion and eventually turn up decipherable and unharmed, 123 years ago, in the bottom of Miss Middleton's trunk at Skaneateles, along with all those other priceless antiquities that Miss Middleton had no business to possess and couldn't account for? The twenty-fifth-century storytellers manifestly knew nothing about it; it simply turns up to demonstrate that their word-of-mouth tradition had a basis in fact. Like Schliemann in windy Troy, decently proving a few thousand years later what the poets knew all along, that Helen was fair.

"You all right, Boss?"

"I'm all right. I have these times—never mind. I'm all right now." Claudius knocked.

"That wasn't very loud," said Bellamy. "They could be upstairs or sound asleep. Quit pawing me, Cay-luh!"

It had seemed to Claudius that his knock was reasonably loud. The people who lived here ought to be aware of visitors by this time unless they were deaf, drunk or gone away. Or all of them monsters and half-wits. He knocked again more heavily.

(And by the way, are we ever going to get rid of the antique Christian calendar? Twenty-sixth, twenty-seventh—sheer absurdities in the modern perspective. At the very least we ought to add an arbitrary 5,000 years, so as to start the uproar somewhere near the 1st Dynasty of Egypt. True, nobody wants to toil through all the mass of surviving literature changing figure 2s into 7s, 1s into 6s; still, it's not as if this were *hard* work. There are large numbers of retired professors of conchology, ex-secetaries of the Bureau of Mines and Fisheries, putters of starch into perfectly good shirts, criminals, diplomats, high-school children, all of whom might well be detached from their present state of otiose hebetude and pandiculation, and kept useful and happy changing 2s into 7s. Or, the more advanced ones, 1s into 6s.)

Monsters and half-wits, or afraid of answering the summons, and that wouldn't be unnatural, at midnight and under the full May moon. But now Claudius could see moving light and the shifting of shadows. He noticed Ethan trying to peer in through the barred window. "Oh hell, don't do that, Eth. It was considered rude in old time, and I think these are old-time people. You and Ken keep back and let me talk to them."

Ethan paid no attention. He might not have heard.

Claudius heard the faint music of one voice answering another, no words coming clear. He heard the click of a key, the sliding of a bolt. He saw bright green and reddish gold and the warm prettiness of a fair skin illuminated by the upward shining of a candle. A bright-green dressing gown with vermilion glints—it was changeable silk or one of the fantastic artificial fabrics developed in the last decades of civilization.

Bright-reddish gold was her hair, in braids as she had arranged it for bed but partly free at her forehead, soft and luminous. As bravely as he might, Claudius met her inquiring gaze—oh, maybe no inquiry at all, only a slow-blooming astonishment and delight in this face that had never learned concealment.

3.   The Mystery of Meetings

The crippled man said, "Thank you for the light."

Behind the shining of the candle and the girl's face, the old woman holding the rifle looked suddenly a little more peaceful, her lids relaxing over the filmed eyes. He said, "Thank you for the light. I hope we didn't frighten you. We saw your light, from the empty village down yonder."

"It's altogether empty?" the old woman asked. "No one lives there now, no one?"

"No one. Don't be alarmed by us."

The girl said, "Caleb, go away. Go to the barn. You're naked, Caleb. We're not alarmed. You look kind."

"Go to the barn, Caleb," said the tall man. "Go! Go, Caleb!"

"And he obeys you! Oh, Mama, they—'How beauteous mankind is! O brave new world, that has such people in it!' "

The man with the shrunken arm capped the lines: " 'Tis new to thee.' "

The red-bearded man asked hoarsely, harmlessly, "May we come in? It's too bad if we scared you."

"Eve, how many? I can't quite make out—"

"Three, Mama."

"Where do you come from? What do you want here?"

"I was born in the old time. My name is Claudius Gardiner. My friends are younger."

"I have heard that name, somewhere."

"It's possible, Madam. If there's no room in the house, we might camp overnight in your yard? And then in the morning cut wood for you, or whatever else there might be."

"That's kind. I'd like you others to speak for yourselves."

"I'm Kenneth Bellamy. I was—"

"Mama, look how tall he is! Oh, wonderful! And the redhead, why, I think he could strangle a bear—couldn't you, Red?"

"Hoo, try it sometime if you want me to."

"How about that, Mama?"

"I was born in the old time too," said the tall man, "but too young to remember much of it: I—we—grew up, Madam—"

"You might as well call me Mrs. Newman. It's so long since anyone has done so, I think I'd like the sound of it."

"Mrs. Newman. I grew up in a little community of survivors, Shelter Town it's called, and my friend here, Ethan Nye, he was born there. It's a dull place. How far would you say from here, Claudius?"

"Fifty miles or so."

"We came away with Claudius. He told us there could be better ways of living, better places to live in."

The girl said, "I never heard a voice so wonderful."

"Eve, be sensible! Certainly the young man has a charming voice, but . . . Excuse my daughter; she's never had the opportunity to learn the usual . . . reserves."

"Oh, Mama!"

"We've lived here alone so long, no way of knowing what's going on in the world, if anything is. Alone except for that servant of ours, a natural, as people used to call them. Poor thing, he's loyal, and I suppose he could be dangerous if he thought anything threatened us. Ethan Nye, you haven't spoken up yet, except a little something about strangling a bear, I believe it was."

"I mostly leave talking to others, Mrs. Newman. I guess I'm a simple Joe with not much to say, in words."

The girl laughed. "In my books nobody was ever simple, and I think the books are true. You wouldn't stare at me so, Simple, if you were simple. Not that I don't like it, but why do you?"

"I can't help it, but I mean no harm by it."

The tall man said, "The brightness there is in your face! Who needs a candle?"

"And now you stare at each other! Oh, I know about jealousy, Othello and all that, but don't you go banging each other around on my account. Mama would take a whip to you both and serve you right. Mama, please put away the rifle and let them come in!"

"Come in—come in, of course. I didn't mean to seem hostile. Mr. Gardiner, I'm certain your name is familiar. Maybe it will come to me. Would one of you be so kind as to build up the fire a little? And, Eve, fetch me that little wildcat neckpiece, will you, dear? April is a chilly time for old people."

"It's May, Mama. Oh, Claudius—Mr. Gardiner—your arm, what happened to it? Is it something that pains you?"

"That happened long ago. No, forgive me, I never roll up the sleeve. Your mother will have told you about our little day of war a while back. I was in a city about sixty miles from one of the points of impact, and a building collapsed on me. No surgeons available. But in a way it's a mark of distinction. I believe I'm the only man in the world who can tell of surviving a direct hit by the First National Bank."

Eve ran upstairs, within her a singing, a crying, a well of laughter. Impossible to walk; running was a way of dancing. In the bedroom she hugged herself tightly in the green gown, gasped, laughed, whirled to the closet for her mother's fur piece, already reliving some of the marvel that was only a few minutes old. Time was transfigured, childhood burgeoning in the bloom of twenty-eight without destroying a new charity and tenderness for the fatigue and relinquishment of her mother's years. *Now I could love all the world and Caleb too.*

She had not been far down in sleep when they came, and wakened easily, wondering, hearing the breathing that meant Mama was sleeping comfortably. She had risen from her bed in the blur of her departing drowsiness. *What's happening? What is changing? Who's calling me?*

Nothing was wrong. The night-light candle burned steadily behind its little screen. No danger, no wind blowing.
Wasn't someone calling me?

She had groped in the closet, wondering whether she
might still be caught in some dream's complex absurdities.
She had groped for the green-red dressing gown that
Mama had given her long ago to be saved for—oh, some
special occasion, whatever the old lady might have meant
by that, at that time, long ago. And she never wore it. It
was to be saved. *What am I doing? Who makes me do
this? Why do I feel as if someone had kissed me there,
and there, while I was sleeping?*

Then strongly she heard the voices, speaking simple
English and pronouncing it in very nearly the way she
and her mother did: "In olden days New Englanders out
in the country seldom used the front door . . ." A strange-
timbered sound, deep and yet musical, in no way like
Caleb's gargling noises. It took hold of her like a physical
force. *How could you magic my heart and my flesh with
a kiss while I was sleeping?*

She *never* wore that dressing gown—oh, of course now
and then, stealing a minute or two when Mama didn't
know, since Mama might not have approved such yield-
ing to a mood or vanity or whatever it was. No denying
there was delight in seeing the red gold of her hair lie living against the iridescent changes of a gown fit for a
princess. *And so I am, sir: I am beautiful.*

Her fingers had found the fabric quickly in the dim-
ness, and she had put it on and stood by the window pant-
ing and trembling and very much afraid. A second voice
was quite different, richer in overtones, deeper: "He wants
us to climb this thing." So they were out by the barn, with
Caleb. And another voice: "I outweigh Buster by fifty
pounds at least." Again very different, rougher, splendid
in its own fashion. *Don't hurt me too much.*

She had waked her mother then with frantic whispers
and fumbling, like a little girl. She had felt the shock of
knowledge in her mother's frailness, and then Eve remembered that she alone was strong. She had helped Mama
into her own dressing gown, a black and white simplicity.
"Oh, Mama, you look magnificent! We're stepping out in
society. Aren't we?"

"What talk! Hand me one of the rifles. Now we've imagined this many times, just try to remember what I've

told you. They mustn't know I am blind so long as we can prevent it. Stay right by me, contrive to tell me things about them, their appearance, without seeming to. You know—"

"But, Mama—"

"Listen to me and do as I say. They may be civilized, but how can we know yet? You have your knife belt?"

"No, I—"

"Eve, I've *told* you, so many times! Put it on, right now, under whatever—Eve, what are you wearing?" Her small dry hand found the fabric. "Oh, my dear! Well—maybe. But put on that knife belt."

"Mama—"

"I insist. I insist on feeling it."

So Eve had then strapped on the hunting knife, disliking the weight of it, but then not too much, for with the belt of the dressing gown tied it was hidden well enough, and the knife in its leather sheath possessed its own intense and secret beauty—and anyway Mama was right.

"Now help me to the head of the stairs and go ahead of me with the candle. I'll be all right with a hand on the banister. Be careful. Wait till they knock."

"Yes, Mama. But they couldn't have voices like that and still be evil."

"Innocent, innocent—it's not good. Good and not good."

There had already been a knock, perhaps more than one, before Mama began her descent of the stairs, and Eve had stood with her candle in a foolish desperation. *What if they never knock again? What if I rise up—I am so light, so light—off the floor and whoosh through the chimney, little witch, and away over the hills, by God they'd never find me!*

The knock did sound again. Eve's wobbling fingers turned the key and drew back the bolt as day after day, night after night she had dreamed of doing it.

The face was lined, severe, on a level with her own, not young, showing on the left edge of the jawbone a scar as white as Caleb's. The man was observing her with gravity and candor, and something was changing in himself—brought on by his thoughts, or the light of the candle, or her own self reaching out to him—and he said:

"Thank you for the light." *For that alone I love you forever.*

Another face was blunt and leonine under a shock of ragged red hair, a bearded face but without age lines; shrewd eyes sent back a blueness in the light, and a warmth. Taller than Eve, he did not seem tall because of his massiveness. His arms bulged out of a shirt too small for him, pulling it open from the tawny mat on his chest. The columns of his legs had worn thin places at the knees of ill-fitting trousers, where any decent farm wife would have already sewn patches for the poor man. And his stare was saying with certainty and sweetness: I could take you by force any time and you know it, but it's my wish to win you some other way. *For the strength alone, Red, I could love you forever.*

Another face was that of a tall man with eyes the gray of a thunder cloud, or smoke, and his smile was immediate, loving, genial, impudent. He smiled as if one glance had told him everything about her inner turmoil; smiled as if nothing could ever shake *him*, oh, never; smiled as if saying: See, love, all I need do is smile to make you desire me. *What am I to do?*

The man with the old face was saying more simple and ordinary things, so far as Eve's dizziness would let her understand them—something about seeing the light, something about the dead village in the valley, and her mother made some dark inquiry.

Near the tall man at whom she dared not look Caleb had been stumbling about, fawning on that man, Caleb bare to his dirty hide, abject and drooling. These were men—poor Caleb, poor Caliban! She remembered ordering him to the barn—yes, and the idiot had not obeyed her until the tall man, gray-eyed Kenneth Bellamy, had repeated her command in his amazing voice. *O brave new world!*

So here was Mama's fur piece. Downstairs the voices were making a quiet music of speech—male voices with her mother's, pleasantly asking, answering, at one moment a rumble of laughter. *The new voices can do that too!*

Eve would have liked to halt for an indefinite time at the shadowy top of the stairs, poised in secrecy, listening like an excited child and growing familiar with the miracle. *But now I am not a child. Understood?*

The blind woman heard a question, unaggressive and probably asked in kindness, from the man who had made a joke about having a crippled arm: "No one, Mrs. Newman? In all that time?"

"Only the half-wit. I named him Caliban, but then that thought seemed like a private cruelty. It became Caleb." She wondered if it had been a mistake to send Eve upstairs alone. But she could hear, feel, smell all three of the men and keep track of their positions. The big one, Ethan Nye, was breathing in the chair that stood a couple of feet to her left. Claudius Gardiner sat across from her on the other side of the hearth, Eve's usual place. And Kenneth Bellamy, the man she knew to be tall, had settled on the floor, maybe cross-legged, a few paces back from the fire after tending it nicely with no fuss. Over the distance of age and blindness Bellamy had somehow conveyed to her the impression of a rather nice boy. "Poor Caleb, he came in the sixth year after the war, the fourth year of our isolation. My little girl was seven. Caleb seemed to be about ten or eleven. He has no speech but understands a good deal. That was the first year I heard wolves on the mountain—I mean the big hill that rises behind us in the west —Wake Hill, we call it. Their voices carry strangely on a still night. I've almost ceased to hate them; they've done us no real harm, as yet. Well, poor Caleb—I heard a whimpering outside the woodshed in the early morning, and we found him there naked and terrified and bramble-scratched. He must have made a rough journey through the woods— evidently knew at least that a house could be a refuge. We tried to follow his trail backward but soon lost it on the pine needles. I think he's coming in now."

"Yes," said Claudius Gardiner's voice, "and all prettied up in a pair of pants." Was he telling her that he knew she was blind and was respecting her pretense? And if so, did that mean he was distrustful of his companions? *Let me have peace! Let me like and trust them, and lay down some of my . . . Claudius Gardiner! Of course!* The name found its twentieth-century place for her.

"Caleb—sit by the door, Caleb," she said, and she heard the idiot grunt and settle himself, thumping on the old floorboards like a heavy dog. "Mr. Gardiner, it's been more than a quarter century, of trouble and loneliness, as I've told you; nothing else could have blurred that name for me. You're the violinist?"

"Yes."

"I heard you in 1970. It's come back. You played one of the Bach unaccompanied sonatas, and some other things I don't quite remember, and a violin sonata of your own. Your accompanist was a lovely blond girl, rather tall—"

"My wife. Were we good?"

"Magnificent."

"She was in New York in the one-day war. I was on my way to rejoin her there, after visiting relatives in Maine, when the building fell on me."

"And on your arm. Mr. Gardiner, how have you been able to make your peace with that? I know it must be pain for you to speak of it, but I have a reason for asking."

"Would you tell me what it is?"

He had spoken tranquilly. Alma Newman was listening for self-pity and did not hear it. Perhaps he had become morbidly detached. Perhaps he found nothing nowadays deserving of his anger, and so anger waited in him like a chilled snake.

"Oh, the reason. Sometimes I need more courage than I have, for my old age. I might profit by learning how others have met the collapse of everything you and I used to take for granted."

"I think you must have a great deal of courage."

That was the musical noise of the nice boy Bellamy. Obsequious? Did he mean his words, or was the little jerk just snuggling up, offering his noise as a coin of admission to this feast of friendliness? Which could degenerate into the maudlin, Alma Newman thought, if her own distracted mood led her to say much more along that line. And what the devil did Nice Boy know about trouble? Why, as a matter of fact he might know quite a lot. How could you tell?

"I have my shaky moments," said Claudius.

"Of course. But that doesn't quite answer me."

"It's difficult to answer. You understand, Mrs. Newman, there are no cities now, and hardly even any villages—just a few here and there like the one where these boys grew up. You remember how only three or four cities caught the bombs. The plagues destroyed millions more than the bombs did, and then—as you might not know— there was what might be called the . . . the relinquishment. A giving up. Loss of the will to live." *Her footstep on the stairs. What's this he's trying to tell me?* "In your isolation you may never have been aware of that. I've seen people die, Mrs. Newman, in apparent health, with food available and no immediate danger threatening—just lie down and presently cease to live. Call it the disease of despair. Or the intangible wound."

"But how *could* that be?" said Eve, and Alma Newman felt the fur piece settled around her shoulders, the touching of youthful hands, the warmth as Eve sat on the floor by her, leaning against her thigh. *She's with me still. Wild inside, maybe wild as a young mare in her first heat, or maybe not quite that, not yet—but somehow with me still.* "How could anyone not desire to live?"

"I can't explain it, Eve, but I've seen it happen. Like a car—did you drive in those days, Mrs. Newman?"

"Yes."

"Like a car running out of gas on the highway. Momentum can carry it a while, and then it just stops. Well, I happened to see Philadelphia emptied by the red plague. In Boston—I heard this from a refugee—a plague of rats followed the red plague, and that probably happened in other cities, nature temporarily overflowing and returning to balance. And I remember how absurdly astonished some of the survivors were to learn that when the huge complex of industry began to go it went all at once— whoosh—a few critical shortages bringing it down like a bombed building even before the plagues began. How else could it have been? But I believe the public had been quite busy for several decades with the effort of not thinking that thought. Well, it was a great structure. One of the pillars was education, and that one was getting undermined a long while back."

Deliberately, groping for the quality of Gardiner's silence, Alma Newman asked, "Any particular hope for the human race?"

"Oh, poor thing," said his voice, "poor thing, I guess so. It's having a sick childhood, that's all. To say nothing of pulling poison bottles off the shelf, not knowing the gun was loaded, snatching up porcupines by the tail, sending in the Marines—you know, kid stuff. If it can get past another couple-three thousand years of that kind of thing it may turn up in fairly good shape for the long haul—there's no telling."

"You're very generous with it," the old lady said, and

with no motion or sound from her, she could feel in Eve the tension of bewilderment, incomprehension, reproach.

"But what you asked me was something different," said Gardiner: "how I could make my peace with things as they are—if I have done so. I'm still trying to puzzle out a rational answer."

In the small silence Alma Newman sought for his 1970 face and could not find it. She had seen it from the distance of the balcony; billboard and newspaper photographs returned dimly with an impression of a blunt short nose, high forehead, wide mouth, black straight hair which could be gray now or gone. And behind him the misted area of all her own memories; but which were the meaningful passages of light and dark in the clumsy amateur painting of a human life, the chiaroscuro from which understanding may emerge even when composition and technique have been bungled?

"Suppose I get at it with a scrap of autobiography. For a while, Mrs. Newman—well, it was ten years: I kept track of the calendar though I'd be puzzled to explain why I bothered—I purposely kept apart from everything human, in places where the forest had already begun to cover man's works. I wanted no contact with my own kind. I have enough muscle left in my bad arm to support a rifle, and I carried one until I'd trained myself to use a bow—the looters left one for me to loot, in a sporting-goods store. Later on I made this light one I carry now, for my own requirements. I threw away the rifle. I survived in the wilderness the primitive way—well, my binoculars are sort of advanced for a Cro-Magnon. I suppose I never quite stopped thinking like a twentieth-century musician with some pretensions to a general education."

"That book you keep with you?" said the voice of Ethan Nye.

"Oh, that, Eth. I've had that only two or three years. I found it in an old house on the Hudson—roof falling in, everyone long gone except Walt Whitman, and I hated to leave him with the rain-drip and crumbling plaster. Look at all the books here, by the way! In this house Walt Whitman would be taken for granted. Those binoculars were useful to me during those years. Ten-power. It's handy to know if something's waiting behind a bush half a mile away. For those ten years I found them helpful in avoiding my own species, on the rare occasions when I approached places where people might be encountered. Until a day, Mrs. Newman, when they showed me an old man trying to defend a little girl and himself against a pack of wild dogs and myself too far away for a bow shot or any other kind of help. I could have done something if I hadn't discarded my rifle. There was a tree. The old man might have swung up into it and saved himself, but he was still trying to lift the child into it when they pulled him down, and she . . . didn't let go of him soon enough. I'd been watching those two follow an empty country road, a ghost road overgrown with brush. They must have had a hideaway shelter somewhere in the region. It's true I didn't spot the beasts until they attacked, but that's not much excuse. I knew it was dangerous country; I'd heard the dogs running something the day before. So I was too far away, and they never had a chance. I think, Mrs. Newman, that my failure there was what made me want to come back into contact with my own people, if I could find them. I have been hunting for them ever since—not for atonement, which is simply another vanity, but for my own welfare and theirs. Maybe that incident blasted away enough of my native arrogance so that I could start feeling again in the human way and make a kind of peace with myself. Not a matter of guilt. We were irrational about guilt in the twentieth century, weren't we? We wallowed in it. Guilt actually sidetracks one from taking a proper responsibility for his acts—pretends to be the same as responsibility and so corrupts the real thing. . . . That incident of my failure forced me to rediscover my relation to my own kind."

"Your failure," said Eve's voice. "But, Claudius, if you were too far away—"

"I should not have been too far away."

4.   And of Partings

Ethan Nye watched the old woman's hand fondle the girl's shoulder and drop away. Claudius' words sounded on in him with their hint of something important behind the unreasonable. How the hell could a man help being too far away if he just was? And ordinarily when trouble happens that's where you are. He looked at the Boss. *What's changing? What's happening?* He was seeing the man as if all he had felt for him in the last three weeks were not gone, certainly, but somehow suspended.

Had Claudius worked a spell on him? And now had someone—the witchy old woman or the girl herself or some whimsical Thing outside and beyond all of them—laid a counterspell setting him free of that and captive to something else? *What's driving me?*

Belief in what some enthusiasts called Old Wisdom, still officially condemned in Shelter Town and growing stronger all the time, had not taken much hold on Ethan Nye—merely enough to render him uncomfortable at moments of uncertainty. He knew that children in the settlement were being furtively taught dark rituals and enjoying it. Sometimes he had wondered whether he might be missing some satisfaction or other. He tried now to shrug all this away, watching the warm woman in the red-green gown, tasting in advance the impudent luxury of the full upper lip, exploring in fancy the dark division of her breasts, marveling at her eyes that moved continually and so candidly from one stranger to another as if she meant to swallow all three in the hunger and curiosity of the blue-green stare. *God, isn't she magic enough? A kiss from her . . . That curve of flank and waist . . . Eth, you never had one like that—you didn't know they made them like that.*

"Too far away," said the old woman, and with half his attention Ethan heard her go on, echoing his own thought: "Mr. Gardiner, we almost always are too far away when trouble strikes. Isn't that a part of the human condition?"

"Perhaps. But I had to judge myself, and the verdict was that I had been too far away too long."

Ethan knew he would need time and patience. These were brain-people, the girl and her mother as much as weird old Claudius, whom he still seemed to love, more or less—and, for that matter, Ken Bellamy had always been mighty much of a brain-guy himself, puzzling his head over tough questions, beating away at the books while they let him in spite of his bad eyes, now and then cutting loose with some deep damn remark that would go on itching in your head for days. Like when he said that

Administrator Borden secretly *wanted* his wife to plant horns on him; or when he said, claiming it was out of the books, that the men of the old time themselves had made the Midnight Star and shot it up there to travel forever around the world. Well, with brain-people, you had to remember they were some-way obliged to talk everything into the ground before anything else could be done about it, and there was no way it could be hurried by a simple man who certainly didn't want to hurt or scare them. Just be patient, and she'd come around. *Couldn't hurt her. Couldn't live with yourself if you hurt a little stacked-up soft-lipped package like that.*

Well, alone with him, and the conditions right, she wouldn't bother with brain-talk. She'd talk a different way. And right now it was smart of her to be giving all three of them a sort of sweet-eye—including the old man, for God's sake!—although Ethan felt sure she meant it only for him. She looked up at him just then from where she sat by her mother, and sure enough a deep rose blush, a soft fire where a man could warm his hands, spread from below the top of her gown and over her face. She closed her eyes, opened them with the flicker of a wild sweet smile at him and would not look his way again.

He tried to imagine living with such an armful. After he won and warmed her she'd be crazy for it. His to take in the days and nights—in bed, out in the sunny fields, the woods, any time.

"And you've been looking for your own kind ever since," said the old woman, prompting the Boss who had gone into one of his brown studies. "You should have much to tell us."

"Mostly of wandering—though I have found families and tiny communities here and there. I was wandering with some purpose at least, wanting to find rather than to avoid; such changes don't happen suddenly to a man. I suppose there's a part of me that could always be content to sit in the lee of a dead log in the rain and broil a rabbit on the end of a stick. . . . I've walked west as far as the Mississippi. Mostly rich new forest out that way. I took a curving route through part of the South, back through the regions that were Pennsylvania, New York, New England. I lost more than a year as the captive of a colony of religious fanatics in the Ozarks—didn't repeat their holy words quite right, but their only punishment was to make a slave of me until I had a chance to break away."

The Boss's voice went on. Ethan was scarcely able to listen: no matter, for he had already heard most of the story. *Look, Eth, this thing in your mind, you're not just hankering after a good lay. What's changing? What's happening?*

Taking care of her, for instance. Working for her— maybe a house to build, or fix up this one a little if the land around it is good for anything . . .

"It was when I was back in New England that I thought of trying to start a new community. Maybe at first it was no more than a wish to put an end to wandering, and not in solitude. Men do need communities, homes, a continuing place," said old Claudius, and Ethan had heard that voice from him at Shelter Town. "Security for the growth-time of children—but not, I hope, security as an end in itself, which is what it came to be for a good many in the poor beat-up old twentieth century. And some division of labor."

You know, Eth, it would mean no more juicy random stuff like Amanda Borden.

Dainty isn't she? Something to cherish like a fawn, a fledgling. Something soft to hold in the hand. And isn't that what strength is for—to cherish a woman like this? God must have got it figured out that way, if there's a God. Of course Claudius—well, Claudius got hurt, see, and maybe that's why he can't believe. I'd cherish her. I'd let no harm come to her. I'd fight off the whole Goddamn world.

"So I was searching for others who might join me in building a new community the simple way. Not to prove anything, not to shelter old hates or special beliefs, certainly not to demonstrate this or that windy theory, but to live partly just for the sake of living, partly so that people could find the varieties of work that can be ends in themselves—"

And hold her fast in her sleep, the way she'll be warm and secure till morning. That too you never had, Eth. Maybe it never happens like that for anyone.

"—and respect for one's neighbor."

We might have children.

"I imagine cities that would serve men instead of smothering them under dirt and pollution and small-town crookedness magnified."

Eth, it's really got you this time. Face it, stupid! You're hooked already, sunk, and that's how you want it.

And it seemed to Ethan that he could never leave her.

"Mama, they must be hungry—all that travel."

"Good heavens! What twenty-five years have done to an old woman who used to enjoy hospitality! Of course. What about that venison we put up? And maybe—"

"Leave it to me, Mama. After all, I shot that doe myself—Danielle Boone, with a shotgun. So if you bite on little hard bits of buckshot, boys, at least you'll know what they are. Sit tight, Mama. We'll have a midnight supper and talk until dawn."

Kenneth Bellamy watched her stand up, the red-green gown swaying and sparkling like a fire in the grass. She leaned down to whisper in her mother's ear; the old lady looked doubtfully pleased. "Not that year, Eve. We must save that for—well, save it. But the '71—we have plenty of the '71, haven't we?"

"Plenty."

Bellamy thought: *The others were nothing like this. What's changing? What's happening?*

"The '71, then." Looking apparently at him—but Bellamy was bothered by a vagueness in Mrs. Newman's gaze; surely she could not be blind, or she wouldn't turn her head to follow the movements of others, would she? —Mrs. Newman explained: "Our wine. My husband used to make it every year, even after the war, right up to the year of his death. I'm afraid Eve and I haven't made much and it doesn't always turn out too well, but we still take care of the vines. I dare say they could be brought back into bearing the way they used to."

"They'll be brought back," Eve said. For the first time Bellamy heard a note of absent-mindedness in her voice. No doubt she was thinking of the grapes, but of more than that too. *A message for me, darling?* Oh, it could be just the problems of getting a supper—housewife-thinking. *Her voice is a kiss in sound. I'll say that to her when the time is right.*

He stood, giving her room to pass between him and Ethan's chair on her way to the kitchen, and he smiled down as her sweet-smelling warmth slipped by—well, she wouldn't lift her eyes to him. Knew he was smiling, sure, but slipped by so neatly! *How could you do this to me?* Maybe he had dropped off to sleep; maybe any minute now he would wake sheepishly in the dusty sunlight of the loft in the big Shelter Town dairy barn, one of the cozy spots up there where the knowing could sneak away for forty winks or forty bounces with a willing wench— wake and find his companion had been tickling him with a straw.

No such thing. This was real. And dodging his look the way she had—why, that might be a good sign. If she wouldn't trust herself to meet his eyes, her feeling for him must be blowing up a real storm. As soon as they could be alone together, that mask of hers would fall away. Then her eyes might still be downcast trying for concealment, but he would see a trembling of her mouth, the turmoil of excited breathing, other messages. With a few curious fears and hesitations that no other girl had ever caused in him, Bellamy's mind played through some of the game in advance—approaches and retreats, mimic and real hostility, the climax of her certain surrender— but in his mind it was still different from anything in the past. *Behold, my love, thou art fair* . . .

And right now, by the way, what about an offer to help in the kitchen? Or had he already been a little too pushing? Was that why when she did glance at him she seemed to be showing a bit of actual fright, even hurt? *I'll never hurt you.*

He inspected the woodbox by the hearth. "Shall I fetch in some more firewood, Mrs. Newman?"

"Oh, let Caleb, he usually—wood, Caleb!"

The half-wit rose and lumbered off, glancing over his shoulder at Bellamy with doggy sentimentality. Bellamy was aware of Ethan's gaze too, blue fire sparkling at him with altogether too much understanding. The old lady's small high-boned hand moved out to rest on the bulge of Ethan's arm. "And this is the boy who likes to strangle bears."

Nice to have the Walnut-Cracker pushed back into childhood and to hear his lame-brained efforts to flounder back out of it: "Oh, not really, ma'am. In fact that was your daughter's idea. I just went along with it for laughs."

Claudius remarked, "Normally he's quite kind to bears."

"Sure," said Ethan. The fierce blue fire was still boring into his boyhood acquaintance Kenneth Bellamy, and it seemed then to Bellamy's always somewhat detached and private insight that this was not a friendship dying but something happening on quite a different level. As though Eth might actually like him no less even while clobbering the hell out of him. Or trying to. *Never mind the bad eyes, friend—I could handle a knife at close quarters.* But he never had. Bellamy had done no real fighting since the small, frantic wars of young boyhood. "A bear ain't hard to get along with," Ethan was saying. "It's people make all the trouble. Horsing around. Fighting. Wanting what they can't have."

"Good old philosophy," said Bellamy. His sense of his own potential courage astonished him; maybe he wasn't entirely believing in it. If Ethan were truly coming at him, all that beef and animal ferocity, what then? *We can be civilized, can't we?* Now was that thought a retreat into gutless surrender, or did he truthfully care something about civilized restraints? "Homespun philosophy, they call it," said Bellamy.

"I guess so," said Ethan, "if that means it comes from the heart and the guts, not from the damn books."

Claudius said with unpleasant softness, "There won't be anything like that, not in this house or within a mile of it. So if you need a war, you know where to go."

Before Bellamy could find speech, Ethan was saying rather tranquilly, "I agree. There's no harm in us, Mrs. Newman. I grew up with Ken here as a sort of big brother, so I got in the habit of squabbling with him. And now that I'm big enough to bust him in two I can't seem to quit, but I don't mean anything by it."

As Caleb blundered in with an armload for the woodbox, Eve's voice came from the kitchen: "I need more wood for the stove too. And water from the well, and the help of able hands but not too many." Maybe, thought Bellamy, she never spoke at all without that overtone of music. "I'll take two volunteers and you keep one, Mama, okay?"

In the kitchen doorway Bellamy ironically stood aside. "Youth before beauty." Ethan passed him silently, the blue blaze saying in one upward flash that the joke was a poor one. For that moment only, Bellamy was on the edge of thinking: *Oh, very well—she's just a woman.*

But he saw her then, the red-gold hair gleaming before the May-night darkness of a window. She was lighting a three-branched candlestick from a candle already burning, the upward glow revealing her face in a thoughtful and distant 'mood not to be explored by him or Ethan or her mother or anyone. Quite aware of them, presently she smiled and set the big candlestick on the table and began giving them orders with homely amusement and other pleasure, sending Ethan to the well, himself to the woodshed. But something of the distant mood remained with her, reminding him of the existence of a self as remote and inviolate as he knew his own to be.

Just a woman—well, there was truth in those idiot words: she was just a woman and he just a man. But he needed her. And it seemed to Bellamy for the first time that the notion of conquest had become ludicrous. Hurt, frightened, overpowered sometimes, or overpersuaded or tricked —all a rather ugly business when you considered it so, in such words—but conquered? With that untouchable self in there? *I didn't "conquer" even Sally any more than Amanda Borden, though Sally clung like a burr and wept and wailed that she wanted to be a slave. Conquest be damned.*

But he couldn't step aside, not even for Red Nye and his acre of muscle. And it seemed to him that this was love, if there was such a thing as love. *And there is such a thing.*

And it seemed to Kenneth Bellamy that he could never leave her.

"I keep thinking," said the old lady to Claudius, "of certain ancient fairy tales, the ones that I read and that were read to me in childhood, when everything was so strangely different. I grew up in a well-to-do family, Mr. Gardiner—in fact, my father could rightly be called a rich man—and I didn't learn about poverty and making ends meet until I married. Daddy couldn't approve of cranks. The old legends—I wonder, haven't people always lived in a legend? They write it themselves. Sometimes they've made it a ghastly story, sometimes dull, sometimes lovely. Sometimes, like poor writers or beginners, they're haunted by the notion that stories must have endings. And somehow even at the worst you keep finding flashes of goodness, and of course never any sheer black and white. Do you love my daughter?"

"Yes."

"I must remind Eve about a little tale in Grimm—my, how she used to demand that I read to her from Grimm, Anderson, the older legends! She couldn't get enough of them, and after she was reading fluently herself she still liked to have me read them to her for the sound of it. Would you find me a volume of Grimm? It ought to be on the third shelf from the top in the case farthest to the left, a worn book, green with a bit of black and gold. 'The White Snake' is the story I want. Remember it?"

"Not quite."

"It's one of the many stories of a tough-minded princess who set her suitors impossible tasks. I wonder if you could say that childhood is over on the day when we know in advance how all those stories end?"

"It's as good a definition as any of the close of childhood."

"Well, the little princess, of course she's older than history, and I'm sure Freud had his own fun with the idea in the fraction of eternity that you and I remember."

"Here it is, 'The White Snake.' "

"Eve sounds happy, doesn't she, giving them orders out there? You might read me a little. You know I'm blind, don't you?"

"Yes."

"Do the others know?"

"Ethan probably. Ken Bellamy is very nearsighted. He might not be aware of it."

"Mr. Gardiner—Claudius—are they . . . kind?"

"I wish I could answer that more completely. They wouldn't harm Eve. Shelter Town did at least bring them up with the minimum decencies. They wouldn't show her any brutality, but could start fighting each other. They're good men, but I've known them only three weeks. The savage is well under control in both, but I can't tell you just how near the surface it might be."

"Well, read to me a little. Refresh my memory."

" 'A long time ago there lived a king who was famed for his wisdom through all the land. Nothing was hidden—' "

"It does come back. The young servant ate a piece of the king's white snake and learned the language of the animals—a nice kind of cheating, I always thought. And he went wandering—"

"Before that, though, I see he was accused of stealing the queen's ring, and proved his innocence by playing it very, very dirty on the duck who'd swallowed it."

"Sure, if a duck gets in the way of the Oedipus thing

it's bad for the duck. Then—let's see if I remember—he went wandering, being rather inconsistently kind to animals. Killing his horse to feed the abandoned ravens—after all! And then finally there was the princess, the other king's daughter in need of a husband and giving everyone a hard time because the story required it. Read me the ending, Claudius."

" 'Presently the king's daughter herself came down into the garden, and was amazed to see that the young man had done the task she had given him. But she could not yet conquer her proud heart, and said: "Although he has performed both the tasks, he shall not be my husband until he has brought me an apple from the Tree of Life." The youth did not know where the Tree of Life stood, but he set out, and would have gone on forever, as long as his legs would carry him, though he had no hope of finding it. After he had wandered through three kingdoms, he came one evening to a wood, and lay down under a tree to sleep. But he heard a rustling in the branches, and a golden apple fell into his hand. At the same time three ravens flew down to him, perched themselves upon his knee, and said: "We are the three young ravens whom you saved from starving; when we had grown big, and heard that you were seeking the Golden Apple, we flew over the sea to the end of the world, where the Tree of Life stands, and have brought you the apple." The youth, full of joy, set out homewards, and took the Golden Apple to the king's beautiful daughter, who had now no more excuses left to make. They cut the Apple of Life in two and ate it together; and then her heart became full of love for him, and they lived in undisturbed happiness to a great age.' "

"Not 'forever after,' " said the old lady. "That's sensible at least. But 'undisturbed'—that's a curious thought, isn't it? Eve and I know what undisturbed living can be like."

"Maybe the storyteller was thinking of gaiety and variety within a larger tranquillity. I think the twentieth century was unhappy mostly because the shaky machine, the whole blasted vehicle, was constantly vibrating, threatening to go smash any minute. After a while you couldn't feel yourself think, and those who yelled 'Slow down!' couldn't be heard above the noise, or they were thought to be yelling something else, like 'Get off!' or 'Smash it!' "

"Confusion reaching the point of no return?"

"Something like that. Well, and this story says nothing about the youth being annoyed later on by a whiff of damp diapers. Such a story is like a frame for a picture, isn't it, Mrs. Newman? The picture you have to make yourself."

She nodded, pleased perhaps, sitting with folded hands and listening as he was to the domestic noises from the kitchen that were dominated by Eve's excited voice. His sense of exclusion was not sharp. After all, Eve hadn't told him to stay away with his glass arm and his fifty-one years.

The boys were moving a heavy table for her out there, an inch or so this way—"Oops, the candlestick! Wait till I lift it!"—and an inch or so that way—"Men are thoroughly lost in the kitchen, aren't they?" said Eve Newman, as if she and not Mrs. Neanderthal had invented the remark (believing it no more than Mrs. N., of course, but it's always a presentable chunk of conversation). After that someone (Bellamy, Claudius thought) was given a tablecloth and chuckled at for real or imaginary clumsiness, real probably, and the candlestick was, incidentally, lifted again. And presently Claudius glimpsed Ethan going upstairs from the hallway with another candle, looking annoyed. The big man blundered about a while up there and returned with two chairs held back to back in one hand. Eve had been laughing at something breathlessly. The sound ended a few moments before Ethan entered the kitchen with the chairs, and the silence after that was not right.

Caleb growled. Alma Newman turned to Claudius a face of fear and helplessness. "Don't worry," he said. "I can handle it."

He was not at all sure he could, sickened within himself by more than one kind of inadequacy, aware of his good hand trembling and sweat starting on his upper lip. But out there in the kitchen there was nothing to do except move between the tigers. He faced the redheaded one, certain somehow that out of their frozen violence Ethan would not be the first to strike. Ethan the hunter would know better than Bellamy how the fight would have to end for one of them if it ever began. Bellamy with a hand on his knife and a flush of dark blood around his eyes was someone unknown to Claudius—someone who had always been there, no doubt, latent or sleeping, handsome as an angry stallion. "Not in this house," said Claudius, "and not within a mile of it."

Either one could have swept him aside with one arm. Caleb, growling and crying, stumbled into the field of high tension pushing useless hands toward Ethan but not quite making contact. Ethan ignored him; if it was meant to be a defense of Bellamy it was dimly brave.

Eve leaned against the wall, a hand at her mouth. Claudius supposed her body understood while she did not. "Ethan," she said, "why? I would have kissed you too. But I see—I think I see—it can't be that simple. People won't let it be that simple, will they?"

Claudius could feel Bellamy behind him drawing away. "You would have kissed him too?"

"Good heavens, what's a kiss?" Eve was smiling at the tall man, bewildered, perhaps learning fast. "All that important?"

Ethan laughed, a dry dull sound. "Ken, just because she's that innocent, you had no right . . ."

Claudius heard Bellamy's knife slip back into its sheath, and Bellamy was saying stiffly, with a note of adolescent hurt, "If the kiss wasn't important I'm sure we shouldn't get into an uproar about it. But I'm not sorry I took it."

"It was important, my friend," said Eve, "and I think I was wrong to let you take it." Claudius noticed that she was again in command, the storm almost blown by. *What's changing? What's she causing to happen? Or has she no more to do with the cause than the moon or the magic bloodstream within us all or the May night?* "For how do I know," said Eve, "in this little bit of time, what I think of any of you, or you of me?" *Here's magic too—she can talk commonplace sense and make music of it.* "What is love?" Eve asked.

Claudius turned at the sound of Alma Newman's groping footstep and helped the old lady into the tall Victorian chair with arms of carved mahogany that stood at the head of the table. In that situation, her little bony hands bright against the heavy darkness of the wood, she looked not only transparently frail and beautiful but timeless. She could have been a prim and self-certain Mrs. So-and-So from the age when the ponderous chair was made, or a great lady of the tenth, twelfth, fifteenth century, when old ladies and armchairs weren't actually so

very different, or what she was, a dainty survivor of the
twentieth, the century which may have been the greatest
of all if you don't much care what you say. "Your venison
stew's bubbling too much, Eve," she said.

"It won't scorch, Mama."

"It better not. I can't abide it with a scorched taste,
and our guests shouldn't be required to." The table spar-
kled with the best of twentieth-century silver, on a dam-
ask made in the nineteenth that had not been used for at
least twenty-five years. Claudius saw Alma Newman's
fingers rove here and there with moth-wing touches, un-
obtrusively recognizing, noting, approving. There was no
anger in the room.

"Claudius," Eve said, "come hold a candle for me
while I get some of the '71 from the cellar, will you?"

In the moist coolness of the cellar she faced him, as tall
as he was, placing a lovely work-marked hand on his
shoulder to draw him nearer and suddenly, delicately as a
little girl, kiss him on the cheek. He held away his candle
(as he tells it) and he saw tears at the edges of her eyes
and wondered if they would fall. "Claudius, the world
that you knew and that I've read about: can it ever come
back?"

"Never as it was."

"It must have been so marvelous."

In those *Notes on the Life of Claudius Gardiner* he
says he had great difficulty in replying to her. He says he
could do no more than tell the sweet wench how her
generation (what there was of it) must make its own
world with all the conditions different—a cruel under-
population, for instance, instead of the gross swarming
of a termite hill—and how with luck there might well be
another civilization just as complex and, yes, marvelous
as the one that died. Gardiner also remarks, in one of the
rambling difficult parentheses which may be part of the
reason why Miss Middleton of Skaneateles put the thing
in the bottom of the trunk and not the top, that he said
it all very badly: the girl's look of loving listening was
(he says) probably a sheer kindness.

Appropriate, here, for our contemporary critics to rise
up and inquire: If Gardiner himself is so vague in the
Notes and he's your main source (you *said* he was!), how
do *you* come to know all about what they, even Caleb,

thought and felt and said and saw and remembered? For God's sake?

The only possible answer is twofold: A) I don't; B) If there were only one kind of truth or only, say, half a dozen, the poor damned human race would have had to close up shop *before* discovering the control of fire.

"Was your wife very dear and lovely, Claudius?"

"Yes, she was. We quarreled and loved and argued and worked together in an art that can't be reborn again for a long time."

"No? But—"

"A pianoforte—that was Nora's instrument—needed materials from just about every part of the world. Ivory, tropical- and temperate-zone woods, special glues, varnishes. In the center a great harp of steel—no ordinary steel, Eve—to bear the tension of the strings. Dozens of other highly skilled elaborate trades were needed just to supply the piano builders."

"Violins could still be made, couldn't they?"

"Perhaps. I've even thought of it as something for my old age. The best violin strings were also of special steel, but of course other kinds can be made and used. Varnishes? The varnish of a violin is vitally important, and I haven't a notion how such varnishes were manufactured."

"People still sing."

"My dear . . . Yes, people still sing."

"I heard what you were reading to Mama. I remember when I was a little girl I didn't like that part about the horse either. I think I'll take the hint of that story. Will you help me with it?"

"If I can."

"I think the coldhearted princess must send you all away. For a while. Oh, not in the dark tonight, and not to be gone a year or any such horrible long time as that. Where's the Tree of Life, Claudius? No, please, you're about to say 'I don't know' and I don't want to hear that, not just now. What is love? Poor darling, I want you to tell me quick-quick in not more than six or seven words, what is love?"

"It has to be lived, not told."

"Oh? Oh? And so words can't help at all?"

"Don't cry! Yes, they can, some. A lot. Maybe more than we think. When we come back, maybe it should be in time to cut wood for the winter?"

"That's my man," she said, and laughed a little and stopped crying and slipped her arms around him. "Already concerned about making provision for next winter's winds. Dare say the boys couldn't care less. I'd keep you warm. You feel good like this," she said weakly, eyes closed, "but then, so did old tall-dark-and-handsome." It troubled Claudius Gardiner's jealousy that she did not speak of Ethan Nye—silence being so vital an element of talk.

"What task will the not-exactly-cold princess set for us?"

"Oh, just to go away and think-think, so that when you come back—yes, let's say early autumn, when the leaves are coloring; let's say the first of October—when you come back you can tell me what love is. Good, Claudius? Clever, Claudius?"

"Maybe better than clever. Maybe you're being wise."

"Goodness! You really think so? You see, it's mostly an excuse to get you out from underfoot so that *I* can think-think. Because, you see, I'm getting to be such a big girl now, I'm finding out that when a woman says I-don't-know-I-don't-know-I-don't-know, *something* has to be done and, bless the Brothers Grimm, this is all I can come up with."

"It's not bad, Eve."

"Ah, and keep safe, Claudius! Come back to me!"

Bryce-Leong and our honest contemporary F. Worthington Stubbe prefer the version (palpably a twenty-fifth-century outbreak) which takes off with: "Then did Eve rise up from where she sate, and, wit ye well, therewithal they together knelt down upon their knees that she might give each the chaste kiss of friendship upon their foreheads and said to them: 'Fair gentleman—'"

Twenty-fifth century out of *Malory!* What can you do? Stubbe means well. Having already allowed Eve to say it down cellar where she *did* say it, we're not going to oblige her to rise up from where she sate and do it all over again, like performing on a platform and stuff. She wasn't platform material. She was just Eve, darling Eve in a red-green dressing gown of changeable silk, with laughter-crinkles around her eyes.

PART TWO

The Golden Fleece
or Maybe Ithaca

1. An Interlude of Friendship

In the morning no anger against Ethan troubled him. The redheaded youth couldn't know it, but Bellamy considered him already out of the running. As for Claudius, what did the old man hope for in such a contest with his ruined arm, his chilly lust?

They descended the long hillside in good quiet, each concerned with the private ambivalences of desire.

What Claudius felt toward Bellamy (at one time anyhow) is indicated in the *Notes;* it's pretty sharp, cruel, possibly unfair. He wrote: Ken means well.

The gravel road was surprisingly plain by daylight. In the desolation of East Redfield Ethan left them—a few words, a wave of the hand, then his colorful, sturdy shape was disappearing at a bend of the road. He would go on eastward, Ethan had said, to retrace their route as far as a secondary road they had noticed a week ago but not explored. "The north is my country. When I was a hunter for Shelter Town I liked the trails that put the morning at my right hand. If I ever farm it I'll still want a north wind in my face now and then."

"I've followed and been followed by all the winds," said Claudius, "except the one they say blows over the rim of the world."

"Where's that?" Ethan asked, wanting to oblige him.

"I don't know, Eth. If I knew I might have gone there to scratch my name on a corner of it."

"Good luck to both of you," Ethan said, "in all but one thing." He realized he meant it. They were all right. Still it was going to feel good to be alone again.

His red hair, shabby green jacket, leaf-brown trousers, mighty shoulders, his bow no one else could bend—the man was gone.

Bellamy thought in disgust and worry about Caleb. It had required a show of anger to send the idiot home when he came grinning and slobbering out of the bushes on the hillside, determined like an infatuated dog to go along with them. They had made enough distance now;

he wouldn't turn up again. He wouldn't have sharp senses or wit enough to follow a trail.

Claudius was asking, "Ken, you ever do much hunting? You worked at the dairy in Shelter Town, didn't you say?"

"Dairy and town garden. After they found my eyes were bad and wouldn't let me work in the library. As if I could have damaged the books." He found the old resentment still smoldering. The lust for reading had been an honest hunger.

"It's your eyes I was thinking of. Hunting—"

"I can tell a moose from a rabbit, good weather from bad."

"Don't be touchy. Had much practice with that bow?"

"Every kid in Shelter Town has to. Hour a day every day, up to twelve. I—oh, I'm not *good,* but I guess I can manage."

"Only thinking you might travel a way with me, if you want to. I'm so used to hunting I could never go hungry in game country. I mean to turn south off this road a few miles from here."

Exasperation, friendship, resentment, jealousy, good sense, fear, pride contended in Kenneth Bellamy for dominance; New England contrariness won. "I might be fixing to go west a ways."

Claudius was smiling up at him in the May-morning sunlight. "I talk too much. Ethan felt that, and so did some of the people I met in my years of traveling. It makes me a poor leader, Ken, although, I assure you, there's thought behind my noise."

Through a flow of disorderly emotion, Bellamy found he still liked the ugly little man. Claudius was a heller— you couldn't use such words freely in Shelter Town; the good folk regarded them as profanity; they should hear Uncle Claudius stub his toe on a rock!—a real heller. *And she called me back—for that red scarf I managed to leave behind in plain sight.*

"Ken, one bit of information anyhow. Ten or twelve miles west of here, a good morning's walk, are the ruins of a large city. Redfield was the name of it. Important industry there in the old days—textiles, plastics, small-arms factories, paper mills. I passed through the remains of it eight years ago. If you're heading west from here you'll have to pass through the city and leave it by way of a fine old twentieth-century bridge, unless the floods of six years ago swept that away and I don't suppose they did."

Called me back and held up her mouth to me for a parting kiss after the door had swung partly shut and the others needn't know—but Eth may have suspected. Held up her mouth not smiling . . .

"—a word I've said?"

"Of course, Claudius. About the bridge."

"Fine. Well, I found no one living there in Redfield eight years ago during a week in the ruins, although—oh hell, it happens in all the dead cities, that feeling of people, things maybe, hiding in the poor blind houses, watching you and keeping out of sight. A haunting, a suffocation—much better the open places, any time." *And when I kissed her she said: Come back when the leaves are coloring—oh, come back to me! . . .* "My thought, Ken, if you're sure you have the time for it, is that in the ruins of a big city like that we might find something useful to you."

"Useful to me?" Most of what Claudius had been saying came through to him. This Redfield would be like the grim ruins they had bypassed not so long ago; even Ethan had insisted on a detour instead of passing directly under those man-made cliffs and their myriad black oblong eyes.

"Useful, yes," said Claudius and brooded on how hard it is to do anyone a favor, or even just want to, without putting his back up. "My road to the south leads out of Redfield too, and as I said, you'll pass through the city if you're going west, unless you mean to swim a river that's gulped down bigger men than you in its time. So we might as well travel together at least as far as the city—okay?"

"Okay." And how fully at home Claudius was going to be in a place like that! But the wispy, dirty fog of suspicion cleared away from Bellamy's mind. It was somehow indecent to think of treachery in connection with Claudius. The tall man shrugged it off; he would have none of it.

Claudius chuckled. "Eth was really bugged by the ruins of Worcester, wasn't he? You know, such places simply aren't dangerous in the ways your people at Shelter Town think. Oh, maybe now and then an opened basement will turn out to be a bear's den, or an old wall can fall on you, or a rotten pavement let you drop into what used to be a sewer—but there'll be nothing in it worse than spiders. A man can be careful."

Old Claudius laughing at me? No harm in that. "But how could anything in such a place be useful to me?"

"We'll see," said Claudius and would explain himself no further but started down the road, saving his breath for walking, his wits for alertness. Reluctantly, Bellamy went along with him. He supposed he must have been deliberately pushing away the thought of his poor vision until Claudius spoke of it; now it was becoming a chilly plague, and he scolded himself for not thinking of the possible need to travel alone when he left Shelter Town.

They said nothing of the house behind them, the woman, the reason for the journey, so far as it had any sensible reason. What is love? Bellamy thought: *If I can't tell her now—and oh, I think I could!—how shall I do it any better for wandering around five months in the damn wilderness?* Claudius now and then offered a word or two about something along the road—a vine-smothered "motel" sprawling over a quarter acre of ground, a thick-bodied oak old enough to have been a seedling at the time of what Claudius referred to without explanation as the Civil War. Well, come to think of it, that was what one of the little Shelter Town history textbooks had called the War Between the States, and a sad thing it must have been. The little man pointed once at a woodchuck scampering away from under some monstrous green-clad wreck, but he didn't bother to pop an arrow at it, though woodchucks were fairly good eating. "Tractor trailer," said Claudius, whatever he meant by that. Slowly morning warmed into high noon.

For the midday meal—Eve had prepared the gift of a day's food for each of them—they wanted shade and found it in the remains of a small building that had been part of a filling station. Bellamy was familiar with those structures. Two had been preserved at Shelter Town (North Pillars and South Pillars), and though there was no overt worship among the grownups, the old people remembering or claiming to remember that the things had been nothing but gasoline receptacles, still it was innocent fun in May for the children to hang garlands on the red upright shafts. This ceremony, Bellamy knew, would already have taken place, grownups indulgently smiling, the kids giggling wet-eyed at random ideas of their own. He ate his meal wordless with homesickness.

After leaving Claudius he *could* travel east, not west. This highway led directly back to Shelter Town.

(Walking silently up that northern road and enjoying every minute of it, Ethan already missed his friends—a little.)

Farther along, Bellamy noticed that the ruins were more numerous, standing closer together. So gradually did this change occur, so subtly had the true wilderness been dissolving in the country behind them, that Bellamy hardly understood he was entering the city until Claudius spoke of it. Then his eyes, searching the nearby blurs for motion or other signs of danger, accepted the change. All right, here he was, in what his father would have called a city of the damned. Yet under the green confusion of vines most of the old buildings looked not ruined at all but simply forsaken.

"This road," said Claudius, "was called State Street. It had that name, this same road, in another city it enters a long way to the west of here. You might wind up there, I suppose. Here's a street sign still in place, notice?" Bellamy could not read it from the middle of the road. "I came by this route eight years ago. Hasn't changed much. Ah, there's a house with the porch pillars down. They were upright eight years ago. I'm sure. That's a style from before 1900, by the way." A jungle-covered knoll at their right was bordered by a high metal fence that showed rust but no other concessions to time. "Guns were manufactured there," said Claudius, "one of the famous old-time rifles. Ammunition too, I think. Everything useful must have been looted out years ago. Let's try this side street."

Bellamy was growing oppressed by the continual reminders of loss, death, irreversible change. Though Claudius spoke seldom, he was saying too much. And the oppression was expanding into fear as they entered this narrow street where much of the sunlight was closed away by vines and trees. Some of the buildings stood joined to each other in solid blocks, nothing to show separateness except the multiple doorways—a road of gaping mouths.

State Street had allowed him at least a feeling of spaciousness, of room to move; maybe the loss of that was what demoralized him here. He dropped behind his companion so that Claudius would not be reading his face.

He could find no recognizable threat. The place was
even beautiful, the sunshine filtering in down a hazy aisle
of placid colors—grays, greens, yellow, the rose softness of
weathered bricks. But you could not quite believe that
everyone had . . . gone away. The vines had run mad,
looping over the crumbling surface of the street. Bellamy
tripped into a snare of wild grape, saved himself, hurried
on to catch up with his friend. Maybe for Caleb in mental blindness all living was something like this. The thought
astonished Bellamy; he would not have supposed he had
time for it in his own trouble. He noticed where bushes
and lesser weeds had torn apart a brick pavement, de-
manding light and moisture.

From both sides of the corridor, that cramped perspective able to smother a man by its very peacefulness, the
buildings watched.

"No one here at all?"

"Seems improbable," said Claudius. "Cobwebs on most
of the doorways. I noticed a raccoon track back there,
where that anthill had covered the sidewalk with sand,
and on State Street I saw something nip out of sight—ran
like a mink and I'm sure it was. Raccoons don't mind
living near people, but mink's another story."

Bellamy hated Claudius just then, brooding on the
heedless smugness of people with normal eyesight who
expect you to see all they do. Presently he was finding
something repulsive in the set of the older man's shoulders, the tilt of the light bow he carried slung at his back,
the swing of his undamaged arm. *Must I stay with him simply to use his eyes?*

"In cities like this," Claudius was explaining, "the lawns
become good little pastures for the rabbits—where they
can be caught and cornered easily too. And wild goats use
them. Along here you can see it's been grazed by something besides rabbits. Deer and goats. The rabbits multiply
like dammit, which is fine for the wildcats, foxes, weasels,
panthers. Seems quiet now because we're here, and a
human being is a large animal that looks tall to a four-
footed thing. It's not that they have any memory of the
time when human beings amounted to something, Ken; they
just notice that we're big and noisy, and they like to play
it canny. You heard those bluejays squalling about us a
while ago—wilderness news service. The place is really

jumping with life. Maybe I can show you, if we stand quiet in a doorway."

"Must we?"

Claudius swung around to study him. Bellamy felt ashamed at his own peevish words and at finding in his companion's face nothing but open friendliness. Why should he mind if the old boy felt like a bit of lecturing? "No, not if those houses bother you so much. Let's turn left, yonder. That street will take us downhill toward the river, toward what they used to call 'downtown.' That's where I think we might find something for you."

"Okay, I'll follow." How easy for Claudius with his sharp vision, knowing this place and its hideous secrets, to dispose of him! Who would ever know? Returning to the house on the hill where Eve was waiting, Claudius could tell any story that suited him. Who could contradict?

What if clever Claudius, right now, received a knife in the ribs? Why, then, Bellamy observed, he would be alone and nearly as blind as Eve's mother, who had chosen to consider him amusing. Besides, he couldn't do it. He wasn't like that.

The hatred passed like smoke, leaving a smell. And when the smell too, the sense of it, was gone, it was like smoke difficult to remember. It seemed to Bellamy that he could not have had a thought like that one.

Except for its downward slope this street was like the other, a narrow, sultry passage through shadows that mocked at life. But it was changing as they continued downhill, becoming less overgrown. Bellamy's eyes presently accepted the obstruction at the end of it as the front face of a mighty building.

An alarming blur of gray against gray whisked out of sight. "Coyote-dog," said Claudius. "Old one, probably a loner. When we reach that cross-street he won't be there."

The glimpse of wildness strengthened Bellamy's conviction that something more important could be observing them, could be following. His strained backward glances did not reassure him. Claudius too was looking frequently to the rear, but would not hurry his pace. Maybe the conviction came merely from the seeming-watchful houses. In most of their windows the glass was intact, grayed to opacity by the dust and staining of a quarter century. Claudius laughed and pointed. Bellamy was just able to make out what his finger indicated, the printing on an ancient placard behind windowglass: VACANCY.

Bellamy's foot blundered against a trifle of cloth and bone. The skull was human. Inoffensive. No flesh for decades.

The vines had thinned out. For several blocks ahead of them the street passed between walls of connected house, and in only a few spots had weeds found the opportunity of a crack. Looking up against afternoon sunlight, Bellamy could not count the stories of the building that put an end to the street—ten, twelve. Was it possible men could design such a thing, let alone build it?

Claudius fought down intolerable pain. He would not permit one of those spells to overwhelm him now. Kid Bellamy couldn't be trusted to take it, being already on the edge of jitters. He remarked steadily, "Nice little hotel. My wife and I stopped there in 1969." It did help, the therapy of finding words, even though it was just for Bellamy. "Come on—we aren't downtown yet."

Something following? Each time Bellamy glanced back now he imagined the flurry of some dark thing retiring into a doorway or down a side street. At thirty he knew well enough that the mind itself casts many shadows.

On the street corner by the big building they could look down along another steeper street and across the square masses of the city of Redfield. Bellamy could see then that the building which had amazed him was nothing extraordinary. A gray tower rose against the strong blue of a river, both innocently small and far.

"The bridge," said Claudius, "why, from here it does look good for another twenty-five years, barring floods and hurricanes." He pointed to the top of one of the great buildings between them and the river. "Can you make out the tangle of stuff on the roof over there, sticks and what not?"

"I can see the building."

"Eagle's nest, I think. Oh, there's one coming, a grown one; the sun picks out the white on him."

"They often fly over Shelter Town."

Claudius glanced at him curiously and shrugged. "They were almost extinct at one time. I suppose men faded out just in time to let them survive. Well, it's nice to see the office buildings weren't entirely a waste of effort."

"I don't understand how you can talk like that."

"Let it ride. Let's go downtown and see the sights."

They follow the street to the lower ground and came out on an avenue as wide as State. A rabbit bounded across the ancient pavement, froze to watch them and vanished in a tangle of green where vines had sprawled over the rubble of something fallen. "I think what we want may be along here somewhere," Claudius said. "Yes." He thrust at a heavy door under a sign half obscured by bird droppings: SCHWAB—OPTICIAN. The door was already ajar with a smashed lock, but clogged by rubbish. With Bellamy's help the trash yielded to pressure and they could enter.

Sunlight was entering too, with gentleness, softened by the crusted dirt on the plate-glass front. Bellamy stood confused in the gloom, expecting sounds of danger from the building, a dark and cramped, unknowable place. There could be dead people upstairs. Snakes. Anything. He heard not even the scuttling of rats. "What did they do here, Claudius?"

"Lived modestly, made fairly good money selling devices to help people see."

"Oh—glasses. Yes, I see. I know about glasses, of course. A few of the old people in Shelter Town had them. But I thought they had to be specially made for each person who used them, and nobody knows how to do that any more."

"True. However—" Claudius was rummaging, opening dusty cabinets—"however under the progressive conditions of modern life it's possible to be satisfied with one or two things slightly less than perfect. Try these."

In the lenses the world went mad. Bellamy cried out and flung them away. "What are you doing to me?"

"Trial and error, kid. Those don't fit, that's all. So try these."

Once again ashamed, Bellamy tried them, and again cried out, but in astonished delight. And there was a twinge of fear. "Isn't this sorcery?"

"It's no more than others can see all the time." Claudius had spoken distantly, almost harshly. But staring through the dull window of the store, finding the world for the first time with clear edges and the brilliance of precision, Bellamy had no time to think about that. Claudius added a question: "Is it good?"

Reluctantly Bellamy looked away from the street and discovered as much to amaze him within the dingy shop. How could he have lived all his years and never enjoyed the marvel of a cobweb struck by sunlight? Or the plain joy of *seeing*, ten feet distant, the shadow-division of wall against wall, the neatness of a chair, the grain of a wood panel? "Claudius, I—"

"Never mind. I suggest now, better try out a dozen or more till you're certain you have the ones that suit you best. They break easily—carry a spare. This is a case designed to hold them." The little man frowned through a pair he was holding up to his own eyes. "Might use these myself for reading. Think I will. Getting old." He found another case for them and slipped them into his pocket.

"Claudius—"

"We'll separate here, Ken. We go different ways. I'm heading south. If we stayed together we'd rub each other the wrong way, and I have some lonely thinking ahead of me. So have you. Keep track of the calendar. See you on the first of October. And good luck." He held out his hand, knowing that Bellamy would have to find his own road from here on. Distrusting his own words, he said, "If there was something good about the kind of seeing you had before, Ken, it's easy to take them off."

Bellamy shrugged himself free of a trance and stepped outside. Claudius was already far down the street. Bellamy watched him, partly for the joy of being able to do so. Two hundred, three hundred feet away, diminishing, still unmistakably Claudius, the knapsack, binocular case, the jut of a light bow. Watching until a bend of the street took Claudius away altogether, Bellamy also saw that the west was darkening with thunderheads—saw their sullen grandeur as he had never imagined seeing it. At his feet a breeze swirled a nebula of ancient dust. He encountered the knowledge that he was alone.

2. The Journey of Kenneth Bellamy

The rabbit emerged from the green mound across the street, nosed about, nibbled, raised itself to search the world, its jaws munching sideways. Bellamy inched back into shadow and prepared his bow. With such vision it was impossible to miss.

He ran across the street to pick up the little corpse. Archery had always been a frustration and despair. So no more. He let the body bleed out and tied it to the belt of his trousers.

Terror had receded but not gone; it waited like the confusion he found when he turned his eyes far to left or right and thus lost his new vision. He was not free to enjoy the miracle of sight. The city mumbled and sighed —oh, merely the breeze, the light May breeze that would be rumpling hair and skirts at Shelter Town; but here it could whine with a resonance like anger across black openings of broken glass.

Walking south a few blocks, he found the gray tower he had noticed from the higher ground. It faced a small green area that had become jungle; beyond that the bridge was a line of beauty reaching across bright water. He looked back. The windows were just windows. He found the eagle's nest. Goodbye to Redfield. Heading for the bridge, he ducked under low branches below the tower and found the woman standing directly in his path.

It was a mad and strangely tinted face, gazing into him as if the dark wide eyes were trying to penetrate a thousand years. She was clutching a wide black hat that flaunted an artificial pink rose. She said, "How could you make me wait this long? Darling, my darling, you should be ashamed!"

She wore a jacket of lustrous brown fur, nothing like the good homely rabbit pelts that were cured and used at Shelter Town. Above it slanted the big black hat, gripped by her thin hand because the wind was becoming insistent, plucking at the hat's brim, pressing a flame-colored dress against her lean, graceful body. Unlike the fur, the dress was unkempt, spotted, stained. Bellamy gaped at her shoes, pointed things with heels so tall that her feet entered them at an impossible slant, and her weight must all be shoving against the squeezed ends of her toes. She might be crippled in some way that rendered the ugly and cruel device necessary, yet she held herself as though accustomed to it. Her tragic smile was a trembling of scarlet lips between cheeks of porcelain white; it drew wrinkles around blackened eyelashes and deep eye hollows that were tinted a spectral blue. "You even forgot my birthday, Jimmy."

"Well, I—".

"What am I to do with you? But it doesn't matter, darling, now you've come back to me."

Eve said: "Come back to me! . . ."

He felt the dread of witchcraft and of madness. But as the woman approached him with that nakedly loving smile, something prevented him from recoiling at her touch. She took hold of his sweaty shirt, a slight, feeble woman and not tall. Under the hat her hair showed streakily reddish and gray. Unpainted, she might look no older than Administrator Borden's sister, who was said to be forty-five. Women painted themselves in the old time, he knew; even in the present, Shelter Town moralists snarled at young girls for dabbing flour on their cheeks to prevent shininess. But these blackened eyelashes? This unholy blue? "What have you done to your face?"

"What?" She lowered her eyes, one hand still at his shirt, the other crumpling the hat brim; he heard straw crackle. She said with care, slowly, "You're much too cruel."

"No, no! I only meant—the custom where I come from —I mean, you must be making a mistake about me; you see I—"

"Jimmy, stop it! Don't jabber so—you make my head spin; it doesn't matter. You were always cruel, from not thinking. But *that!* To be gone so long, and then say— no, it doesn't matter; please, it doesn't matter!" Her arms went around him tightly. The wind snatched her hat, swirled it to nowhere, blew her perfumed hair across his cheeks. "Never mind that idiot thing. I picked it up at Stacey's for almost nothing. You never liked floppy hats anyway, did you, Jimmy? Doesn't matter—oh, now I'll *really* go shopping!" Her laugh bubbled and died. "The way women celebrate—oh, Jimmy, I can't believe it, I . . . I . . . I . . ."

"Sure," he said to comfort her. "Sure."

She touched the dead rabbit. "Killing those little things, Jimmy? No need of that. Everything's in cans, silly. Why, I must've put away thousands. Mr. Gunderson in the next apartment—you remember him—well, he moved away in the—the trouble we've been having, you know? He said I could use his place for storage, so I do. Even firewood and—and so on—only of course I put away his carpets and things to be safe." Her voice soared, sagged, cracked and broke again on the brief sickness of a giggle. "And of course I've done some foraging. You see, *everybody* does it now. So many houses unoccupied, you know? It's supposed to be a little weeny bit *daring*, but everybody *is* doing it even if they won't admit it. Jimmy, Jimmy—your mouth."

It seemed to him that no one could have refused her the pretense. He would have to be Jimmy. The paint on her lips had a not unpleasant waxen taste. The compulsive talk went on: "I don't think foraging is *bad*, though I do happen to know some people are using those empty houses for—oh, well, nobody seems to know just when the city water will be turned on again. I suppose if people simply *aren't* civilized you just can't blame them. I've been taking care of everything, Jimmy—you'll be pleased. I've been investing, see, in a lot of *permanent* things—jewelry and like that—because everyone knows it's *always* valuable, better than money in the bank. But of course that too —don't worry, the check goes off every week to Bruce and Wayland—"

"I—"

"Our *brokers*, dear. You couldn't have forgotten. Oh, and you'll laugh when I tell you how I got more of their mailing envelopes when what I had gave out. They stopped acknowledging, you see—so careless. Well, I marched right into their downtown office here and *took* some! Nobody around. Wasn't that a howl? Not even a receptionist. Well, it was the noon hour, to be sure. All I had to do was grab a handful. I mean, what's the sense wasting postage when you can get those envelopes with the funny bars—oh, Jimmy, let's go home! Come to think, the water —we have to get water from the river now—isn't it disgraceful? I set down my pail over there when I heard something pushing through the branches. Wouldn't you think they could at least keep *them* trimmed? But oh, no, not them—and, dear God, it was you!"

He could not run away. He took up her pail of water. She laced both hands about his free arm, leaning against him in her hobbling walk with those unlikely shoes, and guided him for several blocks into a region where separate houses alternated with piles of windowed masonry five or six stories tall. She said once, shyly, "You've changed a bit, Jimmy. Want to know how come I was all dressed up like this?"

"Tell me."

"Done it every day since you went away, just thinking that might be the day you'd come back. Don't you call me anything nowadays? Remember how you used to call me Chick? But I always like Grace better—I mean, a person's real name, it sort of makes you feel more—more solid like, doesn't it? I never did want to call you anything but Jimmy—*my* James Anderson Silver, Esquire."

"Grace . . ."

"Love me a little?"

"Of course." There was even truth in that. He could not remain long with her—a few hours, a few days, and then he must escape in whatever way might harm her least in her madness—but while he did remain there could be one of the many experiences deserving the name of love. Someone, Bellamy knew, always got hurt. Shelter Town had been varied enough to teach him that much in his early teens. Perhaps a population of half a dozen, or less, would be enough.

Could she be pretending madness, or partly pretending? Could the mind spin madness for a protective curtain and yet stay intelligently aware of the deception— able to patch the curtain or let it shift slightly to close off too much everyday truth? Was that or something close to it the very definition of madness? Bellamy felt himself advancing into deep waters—and almost welcomed it, because so far at least he seemed to be unafraid.

Admittedly the episode comes to us filtered through at least two minds—Bellamy's and Gardiner's, for Gardiner jotted down his impression of what Bellamy told him, in the *Notes*. Yet it may be fortunate that no provably genuine written comments of Bellamy himself survived to turn up with their inevitable contradictions and variations in the trunk of the eclectic Miss Middleton* of Skaneateles. They could only have given rise to more versions of the legend, perhaps none too good.

* Very possibly a distant relative of that Dr. Middleton who, having in 1749 composed a certain Free Inquiry into the miracles claimed by, and implicitly into the character of, the primitive Christian Church, and having died the year thereafter, though not necessarily as a consequence of his scholarly pursuits, received a pat on the back from no less a hand than that, albeit the left one, of Edward Gibbon. Or, very possibly, not.

Grace with the light pressures of her hands had certainly been telling him what way to turn at the street corners. She had been pitiably obvious with those names; what could that be except a way of saying: Help me with my make-believe!

He wondered how much he understood his own make-believes. It was not make-believe that last night he had fallen in love with ripe and delicious Eve Newman, who said to all of them: "Go away a little while and come back with some words to tell me what is love." Words, she said; and since words could be only a little part of her need, was that her make-believe?

"Ah, Jimmy, you were always the quiet sort. Remember how I used to pester you for not talking enough? Maybe I've changed too, some. You mustn't think I don't understand, Jimmy. Amnesia is nothing to be ashamed of. You know the word, don't you, dear? It just means a lapse of memory. If you find things are sort of . . . gone, why, just give me a hint and I'll fill you in. I'm sure it will all come back to you soon."

Oh, lordy, sure, if she needed to have him a little mad with loss of memory, he would be a little mad. The pail of water in his hand wasn't make-believe. It wasn't make-believe that his marvelous acute vision had shown him some long-bodied little thing—weasel maybe—darting out of sight two blocks away, so far away that without the glasses he would not have seen so much as a blur.

Grace guided him to one of those ponderous buildings —they called them apartment houses, he remembered. It was of yellow brick, vine-covered, nearly all its windows intact. "We have to keep this front door closed," Grace said, "though it doesn't have to be locked. You remember how fussy they always were about it."

Probably "they" existed only in her mind, yet the remark was a chilling one, giving Bellamy the first wincing of fear he had experienced since the fear of Grace herself had been dissolved by her kiss.

"I had to oil the hinges myself a while ago," she said. "I couldn't abide the squeak, and the janitor won't do a blessed thing these days, if you can even find the miserable old so-and-so. I suspect he's holed up drunk practically all the time."

As he shut the door behind them Bellamy was startled by the surge of his lust for her. Was there sorcery after

all, pulling him into a witch's nest? Her perfume suggested
no flower he had ever known. Still it seemed to Bellamy
that the last of his always dubious belief in magic had
drained away when he put on those glasses in Schwab's
store. Good workmen, poets, thinkers, builders, inventors,
storytellers—those were the only true sorcerers. *Help me
with more than make-believe!*

The inner hall was chilly and stale, and dim from the
dirt on the windows. "You see," she said, "he simply
doesn't keep things up any more." Bellamy had seen a
few divans and massive chairs like these in Shelter Town;
their filling was evidently some material unattractive to
rats, for they had gnawed only a little at the covering
fabrics. "Second floor—oh dear, don't mind me, Jimmy,
I know you really do remember." Except for its several
secret-faced doorways, the cool upper hallway was reas-
suring. "Jimmy, you must throw away that horrid bloody
thing. That window there, dear, down the hall—that's
where the cans and junk go, to be carted away, if they
ever get around to it."

"But—"

"I will not have that thing in the apartment." She
spoke thinly, shrewishly; a tiny blur of stammering suggested she had almost said "my apartment." But she was
smiling also and close to tears. "Next door we've got cans
and *cans,* Jimmy, like I told you, all we can ever use. I
haven't just been sitting on my hands, you know."

Down the hall, Bellamy opened the window above a
mountain of empty cans that gave off a sickly stench.
The carting away was make-believe, the cans were not.
He tossed out the rabbit. It didn't matter; with his new
vision he could shoot one any time. Bold in the daylight, a
rat picking his way across the cans peered up meanly
and unafraid. "Close the window good, Jimmy. The gar-
bage people are so bad about it lately, things smell a bit
sometimes. Now come in. Now we'll shut away the
world."

The apartment was clean and its windows. Bellamy
thought of the water she must have fetched wearily from
the river—in the winters too—how many years? "Of
course, dear, the power is still off, but there's a special
kind of TV—I had it put in only a little while ago. Hope
that was all right, Jimmy. I sort of wanted it for you because you always liked the old kind so much. You—well,

see, you sort of help it out with candles. It gets real pretty. The candles is . . . audience participation, see? I'll show you how it works after a while."

She sought his embrace blindly. He held her, whispering some of the words that can be whispered in moments of anticipation, unaffected by the shifting of centuries. "Stay here a minute, sweetheart," she said. "I'd like a little time to pretty up." She pushed him into a chair, kicked off her shoes—nothing too wrong with her feet that he could see, except the distortion you might expect —and ran out of the room. He heard her scream.

The dry wail was still tearing at her throat when he reached her. He brushed past her into the bedroom, drawing his knife at sight of the three motionless figures.

"They broke in, damn them! Spies! Oh, Jimmy, be *careful!*"

The three men never moved. One sprawled lewdly on her bed, another was simpering in a chair; the third stood in contemptuous quiet by the window. Grace had reeled back against the wall, her eyes shut; hands clawed at her cheeks. "O God, don't let—"

Bellamy threw himself on them, changing a laugh to a snarl and hoping he had not delayed too long in the time it took him to understand. He pushed up the window and tossed the one who stood there into the street; inside the spy's clothing something snapped, some little plastic death. Bellamy hurled the others after him. Their fixed grins remained indecently vacuous to the end. "It's all right now, Grace. They won't be back."

"You were magnificent." Her face begging him to believe, she came to him. "Look at this dress, Jimmy—just look at it! The cloth is rotten-old. Don't you remember? How I got it only to please you? But it's no good now. I'll never wear it again." A photograph behind her on the dresser stared at Bellamy: a dark-haired young man in a cap with a shiny visor, maybe a uniform. It would be Jimmy, he supposed, though he saw no resemblance to himself. Dizzy, wanting and not quite wanting the woman, he wondered what way that youth had died. She whispered, "The cloth is so rotten-old!"

He tore it, as she wished. But when he took her it was gently, as gently as he might have taken the most delicate of virgins. And in her own passion—he could not help knowing it—there was a sense of the dutiful, of a woman driving herself, as though with each slow thrust and response her mind was crying: This must be done, this *must* be done!

In his own quiet afterward he thought of Eve, if indeed he had ever stopped thinking of her, and closed his eyes to let her image come between him and the woeful, uncommunicating painted face. He could not feel now that he had been "disloyal." Maybe remorse would begin. Maybe, lying here in the perfumed stillness under Grace's affectionate, tired fingers, he was waiting for remorse and wanting it. Or was that a Shelter Town kind of thought? He would reflect on it. Not now; maybe tomorrow. And extricate himself somehow from this act of love and kindness and weakness—maybe tomorrow—because he had traveling to do, perhaps a long way to go.

"Darling? Hungry, I bet. Come in the living room and look at the new TV while I get dinner."

Bellamy knew that TV was one of the old-time instruments of communication, but it must have been something more too, for the older citizens of Shelter Town who had once actually seen and used it never seemed quite straightforward in what they said about it. Bellamy could bring out of infancy a memory of sitting hypnotized by a square of blurry brightness associated with hollow or twittering voices and occasionally a few moments of music that might have been pleasant except that one couldn't help wincing in anticipation of the next blast of interruption. Nowadays in Shelter Town on the eve of May 30, TV Day, flimsy boxes made of sticks or birch bark were placed in the house windows. Candles set in them shone through a stretched shiny membrane—dissected chicken gut was good for the purpose—making a cheerful glow till midnight. On the following evening the boxes were destroyed, with a cursing which had become an interesting ritual in itself, at a gaudy bonfire in the town square. TV Day itself—Bellamy had never learned why—was for the older people a day to remember the dead and place garlands on the graves. The bonfire marked the end of the holiday; however, the young folk slipped off in the dusk for games of flight and capture in the Maytime fields. Behind the bushes would be an eager sighing and snickering and often a startled yelp; and by grace of a pleasant tradition which enlarged the Fatherhood of the State and which Shelter Town's advancing pecksniffery had not yet destroyed, the kids were not expected to wake early in the morning, nor bullyragged into making up stories about what happened.

Bellamy could hardly connect this great sleek box and its one milky-polished bulging side to those goings-on in Shelter Town. If Grace had not used the word he might not even have thought of TV.

"You sit here, darling." She urged him into the large chair before the box, patting the cushions. "It's better after dark, but we'll pull the shades and that'll give you the idea." This done, she lit a candle on a high shelf behind him. "Now you watch the screen and you—oh, sort of like think of what you want to see." Her voice had sagged.

He said too cheerfully, "It's very pretty."

"Yes, isn't it? Sometimes better with two or three candles. We'll try that tonight. Well, I'll get dinner."

"Can't I do something—build up a fire for you?"

"No, I'm so used to it. I do all the cooking, see, in Mr. Gunderson's apartment. It gets kind of messy. Just between you and me, dear, I don't really think Mr. Gunderson is coming back. There was something funny about it—well, we don't have to go into all that just now. There's a big fireplace in there and plenty of wood. You sit still. Wait—I'll bring you a drink."

And he wondered, What about the firewood? She goes out and cuts it, in shoes like that? But questioning her about anything seemed more and more like scooping water in a sieve. The TV—yes, in a way it was pretty. You stared at the spot of reflected light and allowed your mind to stray.

She was standing by him with two glasses. "To us, Jimmy."

He sipped the drink uneasily, a lovely dark amber, gentle as velvet and potent as flame, nothing at all like the product of Pop Butterfield's still in the woods back of the dairy farm's south pasture, which the authorities had so far managed not to find. (It took a bit of doing, since two or three of the Town Board were ardent Prohibitionists, hot for grape juice and the letter of the law, but Administrator Borden, who needed a nip for his stomach's sake, had been able to sidetrack the hounds of heaven just enough.)

"It's Martell four-star," Grace said. "Likely you haven't

had *that* for a while. I didn't bring the bottle because I want you still upright when dinner's ready." She watched him. "Good?"

"Wonderful." She was gone, and he returned to his puzzling at the TV. Why the box? Why wouldn't it do just as well to let candlelight fall on any dull reflecting surface? But yes, the thing was pretty. . . . He was far enough into sleep so that he thought it was Eve's voice calling him. He started to his feet, disoriented. Sunlight had died from the shaded window, and he heard a rustling of spring rain. The woman-shape facing him from across the room was a cream-white blur with a glitter at throat and breast. "You were really asleep, I guess." It was the voice of Grace Silver, who was holding something out to him. "Poor darling, no wonder! Big day. I was afraid your glasses might drop off and break. Funny guy, you kept them on even when we—oh, what a guy, what a character! Here!" She came to him, stooped over him in a gust of perfume, that colored fire snapping and swaying at her throat, set the glasses on his nose herself and stood back expectantly smiling.

The blue and the black had gone from around her eyes. They were just natural dark human eyes where Bellamy could read nothing but grief and a precarious joy: no witchcraft. If there was a streakiness of gray in the badly dyed hair, candlelight was tolerant. The high-necked, long-sleeved gown flowed to her ankles, each line of drapery against flesh a poetic harmony. Accepting the soft light, her necklace returned it broken up in thousand-hued snapping stars. "Darling, I wanted to dress up a little before, but those horrible spies—everything—we couldn't've waited anyway, could we? But now—honest, Jimmy, you should see your face! Most flattering, I guess. All the same, Tongue-tied, you *could* say it. . . . Am I beautiful?"

"You're very beautiful, Grace."

"That's my guy. Come feed."

It troubled him to eat a meal that he knew must have come out of those metal cans sealed so long ago. In Shelter Town it had been recently declared illegal to possess those relics, after an entire family had died hideously as a result of eating from one of them. But here was Grace Silver living on them and evidently keeping healthy enough.

Bellamy was once or twice on the edge of asking about

that, but Grace wished to talk of love. After the meal they sat on at the little table, her thigh caressing him, drinking together—not the brandy now but an equally amazing liquor she called bourbon. The diamonds laughed and glittered at his drowsy eyes, and Grace spoke of them too. He followed most of it, with lapses.

"Question of foraging, Jimmy. I didn't tell you the whole truth about that—so much has changed while you were away!" To the best of his later recollection, Grace never once asked where he had been or what he had been doing, nor did she ever mention in years what time she believed her James Silver had been gone; but there were those lapses, and the warm haze of a man unused to serious drinking confronted by ancient America's best. "I've heard, see, there's a law now that makes foraging legal, sort of. It says if the house is obviously abandoned and no claim is made within a . . . a—I guess it's a fortnight."

Bellamy didn't ask who existed to make such a law, for in this frail, drunken pleasure her eyes were still begging: *Help my make-believe!*

"You know, Jimmy, even with our good investments we'd never have the money for anything like *these* sparklers—hi-ya, I guess not! God, this string must be worth twenty-five thousand if it's worth a dollar. Well, see, I went into this jewelry store the other side of town, and you could see how the men had fought it out. I mean—" she closed her eyes, frowning, maybe ordering her thoughts to some more acceptable pattern, her left hand spreading as if she would have liked to push something away—"I mean, they must have been drugged or like that, the way they were lying, because, see, if there'd been any real *shooting* like I thought at first, why, the police would have taken care of things, don't you think? With the safe wide open the way it was? And so that rotten red hole where his eye—no, I mean—well, come to think, I did try to phone the police, only there was a dead line. This was quite a long while ago." She drank and smiled at him in sudden brilliance, eyes wide and wet and lost. "Clear case of foraging—thinking of my Jimmy too. He'p m'self, I did—not as if we didn't stand perfectly ready to make res-ti-tu-tion."

"Of course."

"Like play push-push?"

"What?"

"Never mind. See, I got a whole box of things just as good as this. Why'n't you fill up? Bourbon won't hurt you, not this kind. Box right over there, brought it in for you to look at. I gener'ly keep it in Mr. Gunderson's wall safe. I declare, Jimmy, I think the old fool simply took off. Hell with him. I mean, we can play with—I mean look at 'em now—want? Know what?" She swung against him heavily, her sagging mouth groping for words at his ear. "Want to do something *wicked*, Jimmy? How about we go make ficky-fick right middle street—le'm all see what a man my Jimmy is now he's come back, and then—then we set fire God-damn city and run away? Way . . . way . . . way— want to?"

Too blurred himself to be much frightened or disgusted, Bellamy said, "Maybe in the morning."

She hiccuped and cried a little and said what the authorities could do with the God-damn morning and besides, morning never came any more. "Know what, Jimmy? Li'l bit drunkie. Me, I mean. You're always sober, too stinking sober to live. One thing I always hated about you, you stuck-up bastard. Damned Christer. Take the old— take me to bed." But when he helped her to rise she glared at him. "Get up myself—besides, what in hell you think you were doing, staying away so long? Can't you see you let me get old? I'm ten thousand years old and sick of it, hear me? What did you *mean* by it?" Her hand swaying up as if to claw him relaxed and stroked his shoulder. He carried her to the bed. Feebly she helped him remove the diamonds and the creamy gown. She said, "Bring bottle."

He brought her the bourbon bottle. It was a quart bottle nearly full. They had begun their drinking after dinner by finishing a bottle already opened. Grace did not drink more now, but motioned him to set the liquor on the floor by the bed. "You stand by," she said and rolled her face into the pillow. "I mean bo'l stand by. Don't care what Jimmy does. Jimmy doesn't love me, maybe he don't live here any more."

"I love you," said Bellamy. He remembered clearly, saying it.

"Doesn't matter. Old woman wants bo'l stand by."

"You're not old."

"Damn liar. Come prove it! Come . . ." She groaned and was asleep, and Bellamy himself collapsed in a not-caring haze.

He woke before dawn. In dark imagination, not in dream, he was watching the restless blaze of the diamonds against the softness of Eve Newman's throat. A way of telling her what love is? What should sparkling cold mineral have to do with love? Oh, this much perhaps—that the diamonds possessed their own beauty, a self-contained perfection.

Never mind all that. He wanted them for Eve, and he saw himself securing the clasp of the string behind Eve's neck, the glittering river between them as they kissed. He could not stop seeing it. He could imagine the cool, harmless fire dancing between her breasts when she was giving up her virginity, and not crying too much because he would be gentle.

He sneaked out of the bed that reeked of perfume and stale alcohol, where he must have lain sodden all night long until now—whatever the time was now. The moon was gone, or heavily clouded. Grace was snoring. His glasses and their latent magic lay on the dresser—and the diamonds too. He felt his way to it. His fingers found the glasses first and put them on; then a barely perceptible light from the window touched the diamonds. Out of his curious, tentative fingers the necklace poured its serpentine weight into his shirt pocket.

He dressed himself carefully, silently. Bow and arrows and knife—those were in the living room. Flint and steel, glasses case—everything okay.

In the next room a half-seen nastiness squeaked and jumped in flight from the abandoned supper table. His stomach clenched as he understood it had been prowling while they slept; then he forgot it. His mind was toiling uneasily, perhaps slightly hung over though he was spared the headache.

He would not regret meeting Grace, nor feel shame at the passage of love that had seemed to give her some comfort and pleasure. But he must go now, and with no profitless pain of farewells. And might it not be less pain for her if she could despise him as a common thief? Surely she knew in her heart the whole Jimmy thing was make-believe. And wasn't anger easier to endure than the sense of rejection she would feel if he just walked out? The argument was wrong somehow—mean and specious, or anyhow incomplete—but he could not work it through now, in this stifling perfumed air. Later. Now he would just go and the diamonds with him. Right or wrong. If jewels could be any comfort to Grace in her make-believe world, she still had a box full of them, hadn't she? The box's weight and muted rattling reassured him.

He understood then that his only true cruelty to her had been involuntary and was irreparable: he simply should not have appeared. Her world was too frail for contact with flesh and blood, and he, the Boy Blunderer of Shelter Town, had smashed it before he knew any such fragile thing could exist at all.

As he opened the front door of the apartment, a hint of daylight from the window of the outer hall touched the face of the television set, which brightened like an eye widening in astonishment and winked shut.

The conquered clothing dummies asprawl in the street were too horrible, needing no spread of blood to suggest the aftermath of massacre. Grace mustn't come out and see them like that. Bellamy hauled them into the lobby and settled them there in decorum. The street as he hurried back to it gave him no welcome except an increasing neutral assurance of dawn.

He turned the first corner quickly, wanting to put the apartment house out of sight, and lost himself in blind city pathways until a glint of first light on gray showed him the same hotel that had so amazed him yesterday. Good old hotel. He ran for downtown along a remembered street, heedless of small things that scuttled out of his way. Then downtown, the optician's, the jungle park before the tower, and at last the bridge.

The river beneath him was not yet strong-colored in the daylight but a dark motion ancient, impersonal, terrible; it could sweep him into nothing, as a nothing—if he chose, only if he chose. Or what if the bridge yielded to some incalculable shift of forces? What if a careless pressing hand touched a crumbling spot in the old railing, the concrete guard that looked so timelessly solid?

A rusted-out vehicle sat in the middle of the bridge, tires long ago rotted. Like others he had seen since leaving Shelter Town it was an aimless thing, even its original function scarcely apparent any more. Out here on the bridge no vines could reach it to pull it down into the decency of earth.

Bellamy would have liked to loaf here and watch the river a while, but he felt driven, as if the city could pursue him with watchfulness. Guilt? It didn't seem so. More as though something, perhaps something Caleb-like, were tracking him down with love or hate or both. Hurrying westward leaving the bridge behind, he told himself that he could present his actions before what old Claudius called the tribunal of personal judgment and declare himself not guilty. Or not *too* guilty.

Nevertheless three hours later he noticed he was still walking too fast. He realized he had eaten nothing since that drunken supper with Grace; that pain in his belly was hunger, nothing but hunger. He walked more slowly at the side of the empty road, cool in the still early morning, studying the mystery of the encroaching forest with the eye of a would-be hunter. That gray spot yonder? His wonderful vision showed it to be nothing but a rabbit-shaped rock. Worry, hunger's companion, impeded him. He knew his progress was clumsy, still too hurried.

Glancing ahead down the great road, he knew what it was he saw, for these glasses did not lie, but his mind refused immediate belief. He could not tell whether the distant pale golden thing had observed him. It was just a panther, of course. Puma. Catamount. They always ran, said Ethan Nye.

But—since his mind must sooner or later be truthful with itself—this was nothing of the sort. It was too vast, too sure of itself, wilderness made flesh. It had no right to exist, and it was not a panther.

Without thinking, Bellamy slunk into the cover of trees at the roadside. He grabbed a branch of a maple, hauled himself from one crotch to the next until he was thirty feet above ground. So much without thinking. Then it was necessary to think, and he began to tremble.

A panther does not have stripes of darker gold against the tawny lightness of its pelt. So the whole thing was a deception of the sunlight and perhaps of his splendid glasses? Hunger too—mustn't forget hunger. He had never seen a panther but once, and that was a dead one brought into Shelter Town by the hunters seven or eight years ago. The stuffed head was set up in the town hall, where the moths soon made the most of it; it had been no bigger than the head of a big dog. The golden beast advancing with such unhurried arrogance down the road was a panther because it must be. Bellamy's mind scrabbled at that thought, desperate for the refuge of the commonplace.

Mousehole closed; no admittance: it was not a panther.

The brute appeared at last on the section of road he watched from his tree, just when he had almost recovered the hope that it was illusion. His hand at that moment was pressing foolishly at his shirt to make sure the necklace had not been lost in his climb. It was safe. The fact that he could be concerned about it jarred him into a sickly laugh. The tiger heard that and turned with a cat's electric response to stare up at him through the leaves. He said, "I might pop an arrow into your eye."

He found he had even set one in his bow. Common sense made him relax the string; another second's tension might have sent the arrow buzzing down. Only by the maddest fluke could he hope to do any more than wound an animal like this. Ethan's arm, maybe. Ethan's bow. The tiger stood enormous and unafraid in the sun. In the book that had been the core of his father's life and that was still regarded with childish awe at Shelter Town on a level with the almanac and the dictionary, didn't it say something about "dominion over every living thing"? The tiger's tail twitched, in irritation perhaps. Bellamy saw the round head swing away from him. And after a sultry rumbling in its throat the tiger was moving off again down the road, toward Redfield. The tiger couldn't be bothered with the likes of him.

Toward Redfield, where every day small, thin Grace— mad and foolish, or why would she wear those crippling shoes?—must go for water to the river's edge.

Speaking aloud, as one sometimes must to help another person in trouble, Bellamy said, "Start thinking and you won't be able to do it." He climbed down and took the road to Redfield.

He seems to have told Claudius Gardiner quite a little for the *Notes,* about that journey back to Redfield beyond the end of morning. He was slow climbing down the tree, but when he got out on the road he rediscovered the tiger, a splash of tawny beauty far ahead of him. He thought the distance might be too great for a cat's night-loving eyes if the brute looked back, while he with his fine glasses could see the tiger well enough, the lazy flow of power in leg and shoulder and flank, the motions of the head, the shifting of varied shades of gold.

Often the tiger paused, to watch the forest or roll in the sunshine; once, like any tomcat, to make water against a

tree. As the morning faded, Bellamy began to feel not
safe but almost confident, almost steady, with now and
then a half-hysterical affection for his strolling enemy.
The strung bow remained in his hand; an arrow was ready.
He might have time for a second arrow—just might. And
then he might stab at an eye or throat before he was
battered into the dirt—without any genuine belief in such
a notion, it still gave him a frantic sexlike twist of pleasure.
Most of the time he did not think at all.

The breeze all morning had been from the east and so
was helping him. Once or twice he could smell or imagine a sharp musky reek and be assured that the tiger
would not be catching his own scent. If that mattered. If
it was possible to suppose that Old Calamity didn't know
he was there. It was, maybe, the Devil himself walking
along in tawny stripes. But superstition was known to be
dead. It got caught in that cobweb in Schwab's store, and
dried up, and blew away.

There might be a time when the tiger would turn off
into the woods, and Bellamy would then be forced to
walk past the place of his disappearance, nakedly human
and screaming inside. Idly Bellamy in his present exalta-
tion wondered whether the man Bellamy would be able
to do that. He prayed to the tiger, as if the beautiful small-
brained monster could hear him well and understand the
nature of his need: "Do not turn aside."

The tiger did not turn aside. At the bridge to the city
it halted a tormenting while. Bellamy saw its head move
to follow the flight of a bird, the white-headed, grandiose
inhabitant of the rooftop, Claudius' eagle. Then with no
backward glance the tiger trotted across the bridge and
vanished.

Crossing that barren openness was the hardest part of
the journey. No tree here for refuge. Bow and arrow, knife,
and the dignity of a tall man, for what that's worth. He
walked down the center of the bridge, nearly the whole
way to the city end, before stepping to the rail and
looking down at the bank.

The tiger was drinking at the river and saw the shadow
of the man's head between the river and the sun and
looked up.

Bellamy let fly his arching arrow and yelled.

Reason could have justified it, if there had been time
and inclination for reason. A tiger is just a big cat; so it

can be scared and demoralized—can't it?—by noise and sudden pain.

He saw his arrow gash the tiger's left foreleg and flip away into the water at the reflex jerk of the paw. Then the animal was a shocked blur of gold, darting up the bank and crashing through a wall of branches.

Bellamy knew those branches, having passed. through them to meet Grace Silver, who was a little mad. He ran to them now, silly with pride, and peered through. Nothing to see, nothing out of order in the open street beyond except a few shiny red splashes on the gray of the paving. So tigers bleed. He pushed through the tangle and hurried up to the wide area of Main Street, the street where Claudius had given him vision.

The tiger was in sight two blocks away, standing with wounded foreleg raised, furious but perhaps frightened too. "A human being," said Claudius, "looks tall to a four-footed thing." And on this street there was a certain safety in the doorways that men, a quarter of a century ago, had used partly for defense against each other. He cupped his hands at his mouth and yelled again, and he took a few fraudulent, threatening steps. Limping and snarling, the tiger ran from him.

Initiative, he thought, somewhat drunk with success. Momentum and bluff. Be the hunter and not the hunted even if you wet your britches. (But who would have thought there was any such beast in the world? And what good would it do to tell Grace she mustn't go outdoors? How was she going to draw water after he was gone? And how could he stay, and what about Eve?) The apartment house was up that way, and that was the way he went—watchful for striped gold at the street corners but not meeting it, not much afraid of it; more afraid of entering the apartment house and, when he arrived there, entering it in fear of the shame that would strike him if he did not. Stay with Grace and take care of her? (What about Eve?) Just warn her and walk out? (With the necklace?) Talk Grace into moving to some safer place? But if such animals roamed the present world, what place could ever be safe from them?

Do anything, kid, except stand here all afternoon kicking it around in your head.

The dummies sat in the lobby as he had left them. Upstairs he knocked, was not answered, and pushed the door open; maybe he had failed to latch it when he left. That must have been about six hours ago, or seven—the sun was well past noon. The TV gaped at him again idiotically under light from the front door. He saw that one of the shades in the living room had been raised.

The jewel box stood open, contents spilled at random, the intense colors glittering along the shelf, on the floor, astonishing the eye, and Bellamy knew he had not left them like that.

Grace was lying on the bed, not quite as he had left her. She had put on a blue bathrobe, and slippers, and then apparently arranged herself for sleep again, but her eyes were open. The cloth had been pulled off her dresser and toilet articles scattered. An open perfume bottle accounted for the new intolerable sweetness of the room. The bourbon bottle he had brought to her last night lay on its side on the floor, empty, but the carpet was not stained. Bellamy's father said, "I knew a man once who drank down a whole quart of the Tempter. It was a vanity, son; he only did it to show he could. And immediately he dropped dead. I want you to understand from that what the Lord thinks of liquor, and evil company, and blasphemy, and fornication. And further, Kenneth—"

Bellamy said, "Be quiet, old man. Just be quiet. Be dead."

He kissed the woman, in spite of her open eyes. The liquor smell was powerful though she no longer breathed. All the nagging questions were solved for him. By him, because he must have made her want to die. By her, because her hands gave her the liquor and her own weakness made her want to die. By nobody, because (said many of Bellamy's ancestors and some of his teachers) nobody is really to blame for anything. By everybody, because everybody is to blame, which adds up to the same futility. By chance, because we live and breed and die only by courtesy of chance.

The worst of it, he found—sitting on the floor with his head on his knees and quite unable to weep—the worst of it was that he knew himself to be glad that she was dead and knew that he would always remember that sickly human gladness and somehow live with it.

Later, almost ready to go, Bellamy allowed himself a glance into the apartment next door. Mr. Gunderson wouldn't be coming back. Grace had been truthful about the cans; an entire room was packed with them. He could return for some if necessary, but he did not think he would have to. The room with the fireplace, Grace's kitchen, also contained a bed, with blankets and three rich fur coats, like the one she had worn but battered with use. Her winter quarters, he supposed. And the wood supply consisted entirely of broken furniture. She must have spent a great part of her days foraging for that. Apparently the only tool she had used was a small hatchet, and she had not understood how to sharpen it; it looked as though the chairs and bed and tables had been pounded to pieces. It angered him somehow, the mystery of it, that born and brought up in a time of incredible skills, of a technology that (Claudius said) was not likely to be restored in a thousand years, she couldn't sharpen a hatchet. The little tool seemed to be fine metal. He slung it on his belt, partly for a keepsake.

In the *Notes,* Gardiner mentions seeing and handling it. Made in America.

There were also many small cartons of paper matches. The word "match" on the label was known to Bellamy, otherwise they might have puzzled him, for Shelter Town had lacked the facilities for making any. The Planners of Shelter Town (who might in time be deified, depending on what way the religious tail happened to wag the psychological dog) had foreseen this possibility and provided careful instructions about flint and steel. Bellamy slipped two cartons into his knapsack.

Rather sick then, at any rate hurting inside, and intelligently afraid of the rats, Bellamy took a candle down to the lower regions of the building. He had no belief in the existence of the "janitor" she spoke of, but someone must have managed the building once and would have had tools. The cellar was foul with the sweetish stench of rats; his candlelight could not spread far, and now and then the nastiness of little paired lights blinked back at the beam and hesitated before vanishing. But he found a shovel and carried it up the stairs, slammed the cellar door and relieved his anguish by vomiting—retching rather, for he had eaten nothing all day.

The rest was not difficult. A patch of lawn a short way up the street was clear of tree roots, and he dug there a shallow but adequate grave. Grace's body accepted the fur coat and the closing of her eyes; to carry her to the grave was easy, since she was most light and frail. But when it was done, the act itself puzzled him: why should he care so much that the swarming mouths in the earth should have her instead of the rats? Well, he did care. Symbolism maybe—Claudius had said something or other about symbolism a while ago; he could not bring it to mind. A gesture. The fumbling tribute of an affectionate, guilty, decent man to the enormous fact of death.

In the end of the afternoon he shot a feather-brained pheasant who chose the wrong moment to run across the steps of a fine public building on State Street. The incised words up there, which ivy was obliterating, were: RED-FIELD PUBLIC LIBRARY. Bellamy carried his ready-to-pluck dinner up the steps and entered the cool shadows. A quiet and gracious place. No bundles of old bones. Safe too. Good doors against wolf and wild dog and tiger. He explored.

A rear door gave on an inner courtyard, a nice spot for a cooking fire. One of the rooms just inside would serve for a bedroom. He would bring balsam boughs from a tree he had noticed up the block, and be comfortable as long as he chose to stay—sharing the city with the tiger or with the memory of him—and do some of that lonely thinking Claudius had mentioned.

For example: What is love?

This is the point where some versions of the legend credit Kenneth Bellamy with an amount of travel and exploration that would have kept him out of circulation for ten years, let alone the swift months of a New England summer. Is it possible that Gardiner's *Notes,* in some garbled secondhand form, actually *were* known to the twenty-fifth-century yarn spinners? For what it may be worth, in the authentic copy that came from Miss Middleton's trunk there does appear this cryptic jotting, which might well have been enough to touch off the whole rocket: *Bel. also explrd after his fashion.*

Anyway, we don't have to believe that he went all the way to the ancient site of Minneapolis, or even Niagara Falls, and shot one of the great red bears by placing arrows in both of its eyes—one-two, just like that—and brought the pelt back over hill and hollow, stream and plain, to keep Eve's little feet warm when she stuck them out of bed in the morning, one-two, just like that. Sorry, but that one was invented by somebody who just never did undertake to tote a Kodiak bearskin a thousand miles.

However, he will have cooked his pheasant, and maybe sharpened Grace's hatchet on a slab of cement paving in the library courtyard. He cut and fetched his balsam boughs. It is fair and pleasant to see him in the last of the Maytime daylight, sitting in the yard and letting the necklace flow from hand to hand while he considered a number of other things not peculiar to the twentieth century nor to his own; for example: What is love?

He was that rare creature, a thinking man, and may well have been the one who worked out that method of making parchment from the mutated oat grass we still find growing wild along the rivers and in some places near the Hudson Sea.

In the morning he approached the ordered wilderness of the bookshelves and began his travel and exploration right there.

3.   The Journey of Claudius Gardiner

He strode down Main Street pursued by complex memories, a small, ugly man of abnormally keen vision and hearing. In the old time, the world had blared and glared at him, battering his musician's ears with the shriek-thump of road traffic and other machinery, the empty blasting and squawk of radio and television, the voices of the unlistening. To attack the eyes, neon, wounding headlights, the flat and nasty colors of advertising—in the American cities you had to escape behind four walls to win any peace or harmony or pleasure for the eyes; beauty and splendor were there in the city prospects, to be sure, but never consistently, never without the risk of sudden cancellation by ugliness: Athena was present, and you never knew when the grandsons of Andrew Jackson might want to smudge some unimaginative graffiti on her marble flank.

He remembered also the relentless metastasis of the cities into their environs. Well, how else could it have been when human beings spawned so fast, liberated from most natural restraints and too vain, lazy and religious to impose their own? It had been a man's mind that formulated the idea of the golden mean, but only a handful from century to century had ever been enough aware of it to admit it within their lives. *We bred too much, and then we died—too much.*

A fox trotted across the street, observing him without timidity. *Good luck, Small Change!*

Claudius had never taken this road to the south during his wandering, though once he had followed the coast from the site of Stamford all the way out along the Cape, and at New Haven he had happened on a tiny group of civilized survivors. A certain apathy afflicted them; there were no children. He had noticed some evidence of more than polite interest when he spoke of starting a new community. Immediately south of Redfield the suburbs probably extended unbroken to blend with those of the next city fifteen miles down river. All one clot of ruins now, he supposed.

The planners of old time had spun remarkable dreams for their megalopolis, the city that was to spread with hardly an interruption all the way from Boston to Washington. Not everyone had regarded the idea as a horror to stop the breath. The many would always accept whatever was plausibly presented, until they died of it. To them, what little the twentieth century had left of the countryside near the cities was a nice place to drive into for the sweaty togetherness of a picnic and dump cans. Or, if you needed to prove masculinity without working at it, to bang away with shotguns at whatever dared to be unhuman. Wilderness beyond the reach of superhighways, so far as it existed at all for the dazed and harried majority of that era, was a spectacle to be enjoyed in the magazines with the nice color photography, if you could break free from the television long enough to tire yourself out turning pages.

The fantasy had included architecture with astonishing beauty of design, an art that had deserved something better than the fashionable sludge of trivialities and greed and meanness the buildings were designed to accommodate. Architecture had accepted the challenge of all predictable stresses except those of human nature; confronted by that, it had to retire, like sociology and some of the other disciplines, behind the squid-ink of statistics. And yet it was virtually the same human nature that had begot-

ten Bach and Homer and burned the library at Alexandria,
created Grecian statues and slapped dirty fig leaves on
them, built hospitals doing its best to make them temples
of compassion and incinerated Coventry and Nagasaki.
It could build anything, that human nature, and with even
less effort transform architecture's loftiest triumph into
rubble or a slum.

By this time, Claudius thought, maybe the suburbs south
of Redfield were sufficiently overgrown to furnish good
cover for the small game. And maybe he would search
again for human contacts, after some of the lonely thinking he had promised himself—you could say it came under
the head of research on the question What is love? First he
would like to brood yogilike for a day or a week not on
this question, but on the primary subject of Eve Newman
herself, her innocence and those flashes of insight that
couldn't, surely, be all from the books. And he would like,
if possible, to shake off or at least understand his irritation
at that very decent long cool drink of water Kenneth Bellamy.

His mind, too, was already doing a little work renovat-
ing the village of East Redfield. Some nice old houses
there. And, for New England, good land.

As for survival, that was almost proved. Men could
live in the world as it was now; some could breed and
beget healthy offspring. Before his comic-opera jail sen-
tence Claudius had learned quite a little about Shelter
Town. Low birth rate, sterility common in both sexes;
but births were adequate for continuance and a small in-
crease. He remembered the Warden and Braun and Kan-
ski families met a year ago in that Vermont village, and
the New Haven group. This summer he would revisit them,
and certainly that Negro-Japanese couple at Provincetown
who liked to hear the Atlantic winds blowing. "Winters?"
said Komako with her laugh that had made him think of
the waking of an aeolian harp. "In winter we just live in
these basement rooms and let the wind talk." Their baby
daughter would be two years older now; for her growing
up they would want a wider human background.

He stopped in front of what had been a sporting-goods
store, noticing the ravaged doorway and windows. The
passage of looters long ago had often been curiously blind;
somehow—you can't ask too much of human nature—
somehow with a world dying they didn't exactly know

what they were after. Claudius stepped in, alert for fox
or skunk or rotting floorboards. There wasn't much left.
He tried a storeroom at the rear, wiping cobwebs from his
face. The looters had left their mess here too, but a few
heavy boxes were undisturbed, ranked against a wall:
.30-06 rifles, with three cases of ammunition—soft-point
bullets, packaged thunderbolts capable of checking a rhi-
noceros. The looters were probably well armed already
and couldn't be bothered. The rifles would be packed in
dense grease, as efficient as when they left the manufac-
turer. He kicked a carton idly. "Hell with it."

He had, as he told Alma Newman, carried a rifle in his
first wilderness year, while training his damaged arm to
support a bow, and then before using up his ammunition
had tossed the thing away in the bushes. He says in the
Notes that it had become less useful, less attractive than
a pointed stick.

He would have been pleased to find in this ruined shop
a better fishline than the one he carried, but there was
nothing like that. "To hell with it." He walked on, presently leaving the city behind him under the teasing of a
mild spring shower. Later he took shelter from bigger
raindrops in the doorway of a motel a couple of miles
out of town, watching a rain rivulet divide at the rusted
corpse of a crescent wrench someone had dropped in the
driveway maybe twenty-five years ago. When the rain
ended he shot a bunny in the woods and spent the night
at the motel with a choice of rather good beds. A quart
of cognac buried in wreckage near the bar had escaped
the day of judgment, as it deserved to. He drank to Eve
and her mother. In the dissolving daylight he tried to
make clearer in his mind the memory of another woman
much loved; but this he could not do, and presently it
seemed to him that instead of remembering Nora he was
at best only remembering himself when young with her.
More thoughtfully, he drank to Caleb, and Kenneth Bellamy, and Ethan Nye. Then he hid the bottle—it was possible he would come back this way—and slept well, and
moved on south at sunrise.

He traveled slowly, wanting peaceful observation more
than the labors and the hazards of lonely thinking. By
noon he judged he had come no more than seven or eight
miles from Redfield—idling along, once or twice relaxing to loaf with his back against a tree: after all, what

is love? And why should growing old sometimes appear
to lessen one's urgency? Growing old meant that time
was running out, and since no man, in civilization or out
of it, could truthfully say that he had lived to anything
like his potential, how could it be that one learned tranquillity? Claudius at fifty-one was not aware of desiring
the pleasures of life any less than in the past.

He came back to similar lazy reflections after finishing
the remains of the rabbit for the noon meal. It was mid-
afternoon before he went on south along the road.

As he expected, the country along the river had been
made in the last years of old time into one straggling sub-
urb, and now the forest was recapturing it in a mood of
simplicity—the ever-present wild grape and other vines,
the spirited thrust of new trees, mostly poplar and maple.
The houses resembled boulders deep in shadow under the
full sun, but weak boulders; this ocean of forest would need
no long time to wear them down. Another quarter-century
should see to that, for all except a few structures of brick
and stone, and some spring flood higher than the one of
seven years ago would demolish them too, or undermine
them so that the earth could more easily digest them. That
morning, not far south of Redfield, Claudius had crossed
a mile of lowland where seven years ago the river had
flung silt across the highway. Shallow-rooted grasses had
occupied the area, growing tall enough so that he knew
the road only from the general shape of the land and
nearness of the river. Then the road returned to sight
from underground, a scarred serpent not immortal.

He entered an area where the highway became a town
avenue, the houses only a few yards apart, and there he
stopped short, hearing a thing that was not for belief. He
searched for decent explanations—wind across dead
branches or broken glass, playing on some temporary sickness of his mind? Some very distant animal voice, distorted? He knew better.

Each gap between the houses was crammed with green
life; the lawns once primly tended had flowed together, a
genial confusion. He could not doubt the sound was coming from one of those nearly concealed houses—that one,
where a path led through the weeds. He had to admit that
he heard a violin.

Badly played. He understood that much through the onset of his dizziness. But that he should hear the sound at all . . .

He cursed the dizziness, writhed in it and fought it but could not overcome it. He reached for support, found none, let himself reel to the vine-covered curb and get his head down to his knees. In the reliving that followed, his right fist beat at the vine, whatever it was—wintergreen, honeysuckle, poison ivy. The earth shuddered in his memory, the blow was delivered once again, he felt the fury of choking in the dust. Then the straining; the stone block pushed away from the crushed worm. It was over, and the damned violin was still playing. A fine violin in hands without knowledge. He said aloud, "Look, do you have to do that?"

The performer had at least a determination that sought to make up for ignorance and lack of any musical sense. He toiled through Gluck's simple and once well-known Andante, with shaky rhythm and intonation just faulty enough to hurt. The excellence of the instrument could still be felt, even through the obstruction of a lifeless hand that had never learned vibrato. The simple flow of the melody was corrupted by cloying hesitations, evidently intentional, meant to be expressive of emotion, as one might dump sticky syrup into good dry sauterne.

Claudius identified the ground-floor window through which this calamity was reaching him. The house, a rather proud brick mansion, stood farther back from the road than its neighbors and wore a costume of English ivy all the way to its roof. The vine had been cut back just enough to allow the front door to be used. Vines overhung much of the open window; in that room would be a green twilight, an undersea softness. Gluck's ordeal was over by the time Claudius reached the front door and knocked.

A tall old man flung the door open, his automatic not quite aimed. His gray-bearded face, tight, intelligent, fanatic, was graciously inclined. "Don't mind this," he said. "It's a precaution I take because of the nature of the times. Are you peaceful?"

"I'm peaceful."

"You do look so. Are you an . . . educated man?"

"I have had pretensions to education in my time."

"Ah! Good answer, very, very good. All the same, I think I ought to tell you I can hit the A in the ace of spades at ten yards. You see that small bird over on that branch?"

"The sparrow? Aw shucks, don't hit him. He's only a little guy."

"What? Nonsense! They're very concupiscent little birds. You can't mean you like them." The pistol banged. Claudius observed a quiver of the leaves eight or ten feet from the sparrow, who flew away irritated. The old man said, "You see? Of course, on account of what you said, I was only shooting to disturb him."

"You did that, I guess. But don't be spending any more bullets on my account."

"Oh, I have plenty. I don't do much hunting now that I have the garden under control. That's the thing for lonely people—gardening! I can things too, live real comfortable. Well, come in, come in, don't stand out there. Be with you as soon as I finish my practice hour—ten minutes to go. Always a mistake to interrupt it. Hope you're not the impatient sort. Wipe your feet, please. I see you've been walking in mud—rather heedless, don't you think? Never mind, no criticism implied." Claudius wiped his feet on the mat provided and entered a spotless parlor, green and vague as he had thought. "Sit down over there, please. All I ask is absolute quiet for ten minutes."

"I wouldn't interrupt anyone's practice time."

"Hm?" The old man dropped the automatic in the pocket of his twentieth-century coat. His faded eyes looked vulnerable now but still shrewd, still with that misplaced alertness of the fanatic. "You know something about music?"

"A little."

"Indeed." He walked away to his music stand, a mahogany antique. "Self-confident, too, for anyone so young."

"I'm fifty-one."

"Nonsense. I don't wish to be, as the phrase used to have it, snowed. You can't be forty yet. I am sixty-five." Awkwardly he installed the beautiful red violin under his jaw and took up a bow that was too slack. "I don't recall your name."

"We never met, sir. My name is Gardiner."

A frown in the bearded face could have indicated a stir of memory or interest. "I supposed you were a former student of mine." He plucked the strings, making no ad-

justment although the G and D were flat. A grand piano
stood at the far end of the room, closed; it would have
had no tuning for a quarter-century, Claudius supposed,
and so could hardly be endurable even by this tolerant gentleman. A tuning fork lay on a table beside the violin
case and a stack of music. "I am Joseph Stuyvesant. What
does bring you, then?"

"I'm afraid it's simple chance, Mr. Stuyvesant."

"Dr. Stuyvesant. There are after all certain formalities—"

"Chance, Dr. Stuyvesant. I heard the violin, a sound
that had not come to me since the world went to hell—"

"Mr. Gardiner, in this house we don't speak of the
world going to hell. It is not only blasphemous but inac-
curate."

"I'm sorry. Well, I heard the sound, and thought you
might not mind having a visitor. However—"

"Oh, don't go! I'm very pleased to have you. You must
stay for dinner, if you don't mind rather simple bachelor
cooking. Yes, I was playing the Andante of Gluck. A nice
little thing, isn't it? I've taken up music—uh—rather recently. It was not, you understand, my regular work before the recession."

"What was your profession, sir? Is that a medical de-
gree?"

"Oh no—Ph.D. I was Professor of Structural Phonology
at Merivale University from 1969 until the—the recession. Actually none know better than me what striking
advances phonology was making over the pioneer work in
Structural Linguistics—and now, alas, the recession makes
it impossible to teach! Why, did you know that as late as
1970 some teachers were still burdening the minds of the
young with the stifling nonsense of *grammar?* We could
have swept all that away." He laughed like the stirring of
a dead leaf in the wind. "And then I'm afraid we all got
rather swept away in a different sense, didn't we? Maybe
it's all for the best. Grammar! One does dread the return
of those kind of things, doesn't one? But I must get back
to work. By the way, you won't find this piece as enjoy-
able as the Andante. It's for technique." He rearranged his
sheet music; incredulously Claudius saw he had uncovered
the second of the Kreutzer studies. "Too bad one must
do this drudgery," said the old man. "Ah, if only one
were young and could simply *express!* But I know you'll
be patient with me."

Dr. Stuyvesant turned his back, his lean body inflexible with many tensions, and sawed at Kreutzer #2 with an eye on the pendulum of the grandfather clock across the room. The clock was in fine shape, and the old man used it for a metronome, although a real one stood by his violin case. He returned and made a second marathon through the famous study, faithfully repeating all his mistakes.

Claudius wondered why this comedy was suddenly bearable. Maybe he was still numb from that attack of his sickness in the street, or the wilderness had taught him patience. Or the unreasonable burgeoning of love for a young woman had taught him some small new quality of compassion.

Or he was growing old.

After an exact ten minutes Stuyvesant sighed and quit in the middle of the course. Claudius said, "I know a little about violins. May I look at yours?" Dubiously, hovering close with a hand near his pocket, Dr. Stuyvesant surrendered it, and Claudius could squint into an f-hole to read the name of the twentieth-century maker. "I owned one made by this man," he said. "Paid only three hundred dollars for it. Do you know he equalled anything ever done by the old Italian makers? And so did a few other modern artisans—well, excuse the word 'modern.' Those fantastic prices paid for the old ones—rarity and superstition. There never were many violins in the world much better than this one right here."

"Indeed." Hardly intending it, the two and a half fingers and distorted thumb of Claudius' left hand reached to the pegs to give the instrument a decent tuning. "Mr. Gardiner, do you—oh, I see. How dreadful for you! Yes, I see."

Claudius' chin held the violin in the familiar way. He took up the bow, squinted along its excellent straightness, increased its tension. His left arm hung out there, a monstrosity incapable of bending even as far as a right angle at the elbow. He brought the tuning to perfection, sounding the full voices of the open strings *"What* do you see, Dr. Stuyvesant? Would you look at my right hand, please? The *right.* The bow is held like this."

"Indeed. Clearly you do know something about it, I don't question it. But don't you see how awkward it is, with the fingers like that? This sort of thing mustn't get the best of you."

"What? What?"

"No need to get upset, Mr. Gardiner. If only you could undergo analysis! That's where the real creative insight comes. Freud knew. Yes indeed. Now put it down, please. I'm a little worried, frankly. You see, you've contradicted yourself. You call this violin valuable—by rather strange standards, I must say—and then you go ahead and put it under your chin with no other support."

"It should need no—oh well . . ." Laughter, sickly and somewhat broken but genuine, came to Claudius' aid. He returned the violin gently to its case and relaxed the bow. "Well, I don't want to worry you, of course. But please, what's Uncle Siggy got to do with it?"

"Uncle? Oh—oh dear, I see. Sigmund Freud was born in 1856. You can't seriously expect to claim that relationship."

"That's all right. Just a delusion of grandeur—passes off, you know, really no worse than a cold. All the same, I must insist that I never dropped a violin on the concert stage. I guess I was just lucky."

"Oh—yes, yes, I see. It must have begun with some association of names. I didn't catch on right away. With your last name Gardiner. Well, you must have heard the virtuoso at some time, and then it was easy to think your first name ought to be Claudius. It's not uncommon. Identification, we call it."

"Well, I'm learning all the time. Still, I was born in Alders, Maine. And my New York debut *was* in 1967, in a crazy sort of way."

"Yes, and then—now you mustn't let your feelings be hurt—it's all part of facing reality: this injury, you see, allows you now to claim that you're *Claudius* Gardiner and yet not be called on to prove it. You do see, don't you? I remember my own analysis so well! I could do you a world of good if you'd just put yourself in my hands."

"It's very good of you, but—"

Dr. Stuyvesant wasn't listening. "Naturally I understood the whole thing as soon as what you said about modern violins being like Stradivarius—after all, my dear sir! You knew yourself that it was absurd, and so what it truly meant was a wish to confess. If you'd only told me straight out that you were in a state of, let's say, unreal fantasy—that's it! So hard to explain the importance of the exactly right word. Unreal fantasy. Between you and me, these things are a lot different than they seem. You daydreamed a lot as a boy, hmm?"

"Uh-huh, especially in school." Claudius' gaze strayed to the window. He did not quite want to escape; in a way, it was fun. "The neck of the little girl in front of me resembled a pink tuning fork, Doctor. I used to sit there beating my brains out for some way to make her go bong." Could Kenneth Bellamy be taught the violin? Claudius had heard him sing a little, a fine voice true to pitch. Thirty already, however, and possibly no desire for such study. "You understand, Dr. Stuyvesant, I didn't want to rape that little girl, not much anyway—damn, something always comes up, doesn't it?—I just wanted to make her go bong. It was the frustration of it that I found hard to bear."

"Well, we're making some progress already, hmm?" The old man smiled. "I'm not disturbed by your coarse would-be humor. You may realize yourself it's purely defensive. And there would have been a fixation on this childhood episode—maybe associating a little girl's back hair with the strings of a violin bow, hmm?"

"Undoubtedly. Check the flow a minute, would you?" Staring from the window, Claudius was unable to accept what he saw. "Just be quiet and—"

"Mr. Gardiner, I am not accustomed, in my own house—"

"*Be quiet!*" He beckoned Dr. Stuyvesant to the window. Abruptly torn from his harmless pleasures, the old man winced but approached; by then the monstrous vision had passed out of the window's line of sight. "You missed it, didn't you?"

"My dear chap, there's nothing out there."

Talking to himself, Claudius mumbled, "Chicago Zoo, 1968—or the year before—ah, there's room in the wilderness, since the time of the plagues."

"The plagues." The old man repeated the words on a deflating sigh; he even looked smaller, to Claudius' dazed eyes, shrunken in on himself as if the word alone had pricked the balloon of his flimsy self-confidence. Could he after all have seen the terror in the street? "I recall the plagues, of course. Does the wilderness actually . . . ex-

tend? New England a wilderness? Sir? My name, you
know, my name's New York Dutch, but most of my people
were Massachusetts—Plymouth Bay in fact, not that it
matters—I do seem to be growing forgetful. But I remember those epidemics. Death so . . . so commonplace. Very
serious recession, too." He smiled placatingly, fumbling at
the violin case. "I should confess to you, Mr. Gardiner,
this isn't actually my house. I . . . found it, as it were,
under conditions that I don't too well recall. You don't
suppose there'll be eviction proceedings?"

"I wouldn't give that a thought." The beast had been
limping. Why? "Have you been living here by yourself a
long time, Dr. Stuyvesant?"

"I'm not positive. I am sixty-five. You see, when I try
to recollect how old I was when my son Arthur—what
was I saying?"

"About your son?"

"Oh . . . You see, my entire family—my son Arthur
was living with me, and his wife and my two grandchildren
—my recollection is that I, in a sense, simply walked
away."

"The red plague?"

"Some such name was given it. That is my recollection. And the violin—it was just here, you know. I had
lessons when I was a child. By the way, I hope you don't
mind my trying to give you some insight into your little
difficulties. I assure you I had no thought of giving offense."

"Not in the least. It was kind of you." Claudius knew
he must go outside.

"This—this recession, it must be quite serious? You
see, I distinctly remember being informed by the university that I would be notified as soon as classes were to be
resumed. And then, goodness, all this time and not a
word out of them! It's discouraging. Of course in the last
analysis one has a practical side—I think I can say that
mine has come to the fore. I shoot little things for food
and keep down the weeds. I still have some canned goods,
but often several days go by when I don't need to touch
them. Of course one's always aware of the creative work
that ought to be done if one could only find the time. The
recession is . . . really bad?"

"Pretty bad." Claudius tried to achieve the voice of
authority. "Dr. Stuyvesant, I don't want to alarm you,
but I must ask you not to go beyond your garden for the

next few days. I represent the—uh—the Survival and Conservation Authority. It'll be best if you stay in the house till we can let you know the coast is clear. There's been a zoo escape, a rather serious matter." *It was coming behind me on the road—limping—and for how long? Why?* "I didn't identify myself at first because I didn't expect to find any of the brutes in this area and didn't want to alarm you. One of the things that got loose is a Manchurian tiger. I just saw it go by on the road." *Now if he just won't ask me how zoos could be kept going with no one alive to do it! But how* does *it come to be there, and* why? "I must get back now and notify the others working with me. It's difficult—no telephone or radio, no mail service. Well, I'd like you to stay indoors, keep that automatic with you but for heaven's sake don't use it except as a last resort."

"But really, I should—I'm able-bodied—"

"No, sir, you can't come with me. The authorities would have my hide if I allowed that. I'm safe enough. These arrows are tipped with a—a neurotoxin."

Nodding, shivering, making no more protests, the old man obediently closed the door and Claudius slipped down the little path to the road. The beast would have to be killed; he preferred not to think beyond that. He would return to that sporting-goods shop in Redfield, assemble one of the rifles, return here and try to pick up the trail.

He had crossed a place where a jammed culvert had flooded the road with silt; a vast round pad-mark of drying mud was superimposed on one of his own prints. Concentrated staring would not make it go away nor eliminate a reddish stain in it. If that was the tiger's own blood the injury must be recent and not serious, or the animal would have gone on three legs, or more likely not have traveled at all. The limp that Claudius had noticed was no more than a slight favoring of the left foreleg. A thorn, maybe. Broken glass. What living thing would attack a beast whose forepaw left a clover-leaf imprint that could not be filled by a man's feet placed side by side?

Perhaps the stain was the blood of a deer, or of one of the cattle gone wild that occasionally appeared in open country. Or the blood of Kenneth Bellamy or Ethan Nye.

Hardly Ethan, who should be well on his way north. Claudius retraced his own trail. Crossing the muddy place, he noticed again the occasional reddening of the tiger's marks. He allowed himself backward glances, rationing them: so many steps, a deep breath, look back, go on. Nothing was following him. Presently he settled into a jog trot that he could maintain without tiring, and looked backward only now and then.

Some hours of daylight remained when he reached the looted store in Redfield, and he spent them in the tedious, messy labor of excavating one of the rifles from its protective grease and assembling the parts. Then he walked back in the twilight as far as the motel with his dull-shining burden—nothing would ever make him like firearms—and pockets unpleasantly sagging with ammunition. He had not wanted to spend time hunting up materials for a cartridge belt. At the motel it seemed fitting and reasonable to finish the cognac. He fell asleep after drinking an unspoken but still rather wordy toast to the virtues of responsibility and the hope that Kenneth Bellamy was still living.

The first day of the hunt passed almost without reward. He found the prints still legible as he passed Dr. Stuyvesant's house—while he was walking by the violin moved into action, rather sluggishly, once more assaulting Gluck's battered Andante—but already a thin rain was beginning, threatening to wipe out all messages. He hurried, eyes straining for the fading marks until, not far beyond the clustered buildings of Dr. Stuyvesant's town, he could find them no more.

A fool's errand, perhaps. He stood in the open in the gray daylight, desolate. No man-made structures were near him now except a dreary line of poles diminishing to the south, with here and there the pathetic, harmless sag of a broken wire. At his right ran the river high with spring, its banks concealed from him by tall bushes that could also conceal a hundred tigers. At his left partly open grassland stretched to misty woods, the May growth not very tall, but swaying delicately under the light wind and rain.

After a while he saw what he should have noticed at once; his mind might have hung a rainy curtain before it until his courage was adequate to accept it. Simply a line of altered green through the grass, where yesterday a heavy animal had abandoned the paved road and struck out eastward for the forest.

"All right," Claudius said. "All right."

He checked his gear: knife, bow and arrows, the rifle with its full magazine. Safety off, one in the chamber, a couple of dozen in his pockets. He tried a few rapid swings with the rifle, schooling his left hand to precise motions that would support the barrel at a critical instant. Given fifty yards, he ought to have a good chance at head or chest. In the woods, though, how do you get an uninterrupted fifty yards? He walked across the grassland and under the trees.

All that day he kept on through the shifts and changes of a wilderness where often a vine-covered boulder might turn out to be the hulk of an automobile with almost nothing else to show that a minor road of old time had wound this way; where one might walk down an aisle of green and find it to be the heart of a village, a poor remnant hardly worth the bother of archaeologists in the centuries to come, since they would be sated with better artifacts of this culture. Always, when Claudius was ready to give up hope of following the difficult trail any farther, some evidence would offer itself—a blur on exposed earth, a disturbance of pine needles, a scratch on bark too high off the ground to have been made by a bear.

Once, studying such a mark, he was teased by a half-memory; it had to do with the tiger's appearance when he saw it from Dr. Stuyvesant's window. Not the limp, and not the soft tawniness far different from the orange violence of a Bengel tiger's pelt, not its maleness nor its fearful size. It came to him later, the *Notes* say, at a moment when he was trying to penetrate the forest shadows with his binoculars: the beast had looked *young*. Sleekness, a freshness that old animals never possess. But a zoo escape would have happened at least a quarter-century ago, and cat creatures are old at twenty. Very well: so a pair had escaped; and so there might be in the present world as many as could descend from a pair twenty-five years ago. Fine. At what age do young Manchurian tigers breed?

As Claudius went on he was obliged to fight an increasing morbid notion that this tiger was having fun with him. Drifting behind him somewhere, rich in leisure, quiet as fog, cruel as fire, perhaps waiting for night when little Claudius could give him no serious trouble. Shape of gun and bow he had probably never seen, and so he

would not fear them. The *Notes* say, without dwelling
on it, that during this journey through the melancholy
woods Claudius did not expect to see the next day's
morning.

In early evening, as he came out on the wan grandeur
of a north-south highway, the sight of the ravaged carcass of a cow moose at the edge of the road was like a
slap across the eyes. Also a challenge, an opportunity.

The body was less than half consumed. Some blood on
the road surface appeared still damp. A tiger returns to
an unfinished kill, doesn't he? An oak tree across the road
offered Claudius a blind at what ought to be a safe height.
He climbed it and waited as the light failed and shadows
lengthened.

He understood he had done a number of foolish things
since sighting the tiger. For instance, he had given his
rifle no trial shots at Redfield. He had hated to disturb
the city's gloomy calm, hated to risk drawing human
survivors out of the lonely buildings. There might well
be a few of them, he knew, perhaps two or three out of
the old city's milling thousands, and they would be sick in
mind, unwilling to meet the present world with even the
battered practicality of a Dr. Stuyvesant.

Entering the woods along the tiger's grass trail had
been folly too, motivated by a wish to prove something
no man ever finally proves even in the privacy of his
heart.

If he failed on this errand, he must return to the Newmans' house and leave some warning, and then, before
the coloring of the leaves, he must search out the handful
of other survivors that he had located in his wandering
years and let them know of the new danger. A very small
handful—smaller than he had cared to admit to his questioners at Shelter Town.

He heard the tearing at the meat before he understood
that those soft-colored, hardly visible stripes were not
part of the roadside weeds. Daylight was not yet gone.
Watching, he contemplated the strangeness—that beauty
should so often conceal itself and trick the eye; that beauty
should dwell in the same flesh with savagery, both blame-
less. His crippled hand, forced into the stress of an unfamiliar position at the rifle stock, lanced him with pain.
That was the instant when he fired.

Where he had seen the tiger, gazing up startled by

some preliminary sound, the dark head stripes offering a target between wide astonished eyes, there was nothing. Only a knowledge of the heroic body, a fearful splendor older than the history of man, gone out of sight as swiftly as light cast by a moving mirror. Claudius gazed at a tiny new black spot in the road surface, two or three feet from the heavy burnt-umber shadows of the moose carcass. The old blacktop must have swallowed his bullet without a ricochet, as the forest had swallowed the rifle's roar.

He climbed shakily down from the tree, thinking: *This is folly too*. He stepped into the road. Diminished by a distance of two hundred feet, the tiger stood at the edge of the woods watching him, probably in anger, tail twitching, ears laid back. Sleek, handsome and sleek with the grace of youth or immortality. As he took aim again, Claudius saw that the left forepaw was slightly raised; then he found he was aiming at a green blank. He swung his rifle to the right and fired foolishly at the dim bushes where the tiger must have vanished. There was no answering noise, no outcry nor thrash of a hurt body. He said aloud, "I will go down this road."

He found it possible to do so, to walk forward toward the critical patch of green down there, glancing repeatedly into the jungle at his right, where the tiger could be gliding to meet him, for all he knew. The rifle was ready with its puny fresh cartridge. He found it possible to halt across the road from the spot where the tiger had gone to cover and wait awhile. He had seen no blood on the road.

Nothing stirred in the forest. His voice probed at it once or twice. "I'm here," he said. "Never mind about hate, but I'll destroy you if I can. And you can't kill me," Claudius said. "That's been tried."

Unanswered, he sent one more of the wicked soft-pointed bullets into the quiet. Dropping a pebble down a well. He walked on north, up the road. After a while he was not too strongly compelled to look behind him or into the sultry shadows at his right hand.

He took shelter in a half-ruined farmhouse, and next morning he reached the junction of this road with a familiar east-west highway. He had traveled farther than he supposed, following the tiger's trail in the woods; it was noon before he arrived at East Redfield. From that desolate village he struck out, not up the hill to the Newman house but northeast through the woods, slowly, studying the ground, on a half-circle route that brought him by evening to the pleasant tree-covered summit of Wake Hill. He climbed to a high crotch and saw the roofs of the Newmans' house and barn like square boulders touched with western light. His binoculars translated a whitish disturbance into a little flock of sheep being driven to the fold by Caleb for evening safety. One of the new lambs gave the half-wit some trouble, frisking and trying every wrong direction. No mark of the tiger on the game trails he had crossed to reach this place, and down there, at least in this moment, there was peace.

With an old stub pencil, on a fly leaf torn from *Leaves of Grass,* Claudius wrote a note to warn Eve of the tiger's existence. She would believe him, he supposed, and keep the rifle near at hand, not let her mother be outdoors alone, do whatever else she might to hold her small island of humanity against the savage primeval. In the last of the daylight he worked his way down through the woods and waited near the farmhouse until the light downstairs was gone. Then he set his note on the side porch, weighted down with pebbles, and slept in the open, not too far away.

Wolves howled once, but a long way off; no other sound disturbed his slumber, and the first light before a fresh May sunrise sent him on his way. Others to warn. Some lonely thinking to do.

In that journeying summer passed, a florid counterpoint to the years.

In the *Notes* he remarks that he suffered none of those agonizing attacks of compulsive memory during this summer he spent retracing old routes and finding some (but not all) of the friends he had hoped to bring to his new community. With characteristic infuriating vagueness, he gives us almost no information on these meetings. *Saw W.V.*—whoever that was. *Komako has aged—the little girl died of a fever.* And of that tragedy not another word.

It is understandable, if he had nothing to write on but the one small notebook that appeared in Miss Middleton's trunk, and a prospect of x years before him when he would need to write in it. What he writes about his lonely thinking bulks large only in comparison to the slightness of the other notes. No more than a paragraph:

"Worst of decline and fall was unforgiving suddenness of fall. Because there *was* true evidence of slow drift toward rationality, goodness, pleasant ways of life whenever politics, stupidity, war, superstition allowed it to operate. In all our ugliness we were better than our fathers.

The following line may or may not be connected with that reflection: "By side of road to site of St. Johnsbury, June 10. A bluebird just passed. I had thought they were extinct."

4. The Journey of Ethan Nye

On the northern road, the trouble in his mind when he thought of Eve was sometimes more like anger than love, or like the two so fused together that the experience needed a different name. Why should he, ready as he was to take her, live with her, protect and cherish and serve her in every way that was right and natural for a man— why should he be expected to _think_ about it? To do that thinking far away from her, to guess, wonder, beat his brains about the unreachable woman-life going on behind the blue-green eyes?

After all, Baby!

She said: "Come back—be sure to come back, all of you! And when you come back I will only ask you to tell me, What is love? I'm simple with ignorance and confused. I've lived too much with words, and still, maybe one word from one of you will shine brighter than all the jewels of India."

He thought: *And I'm too simple, too confused. What do I know? What would I have to do, just to be able to talk in the bright strange way she does, she who's had only her mother and the books?* It seemed to him at present that he knew nothing at all, except with muscle and gut. But wasn't that what a man lived by anyhow? The rest doesn't shoot any bear meat, as they used to say in Shelter Town. *What is love?* Well, he would wander with his eyes open, try to think with his eyes open—not at all the easiest thing in the world. And there would be the nights, when perhaps he could work in a bit of thinking before he fell asleep.

He followed the road through rolling easy country for

a few days of the advancing spring, exploring side roads occasionally, not with the questing curiosity of Claudius but mainly for lack of anything better to do. And he found that when his simple camp had been made for the night and no more needed to be done, his mind refused to attempt anything but daydreaming in the short time that passed before sleep took him. Like any good woodsman, he slept lightly, but in the several quick wakings of the night he did not meditate: *What is love?* He only listened analytically to the night noises of the wilderness, and then admired the simplicity of the stars, and although often the iridescence or absurdity or terror of some dream hung about him in the waking, it gave him no more than a reminder of what his heart had known from childhood— namely, that humanity is full of strange wishes and whimsicalities.

He never took shelter in abandoned houses. He found many of them. This had been in the old time a thickly settled region, and the returning forest was not yet altogether in command. Always Ethan felt better in the open. It was true, as Bellamy had speculated, that his fierce-seeming blue eyes could see more clearly in the dark than most. Twilight seldom deceived him, and he found good moonlight almost as comfortable as day—more entertaining too, because of the wild mystery of creatures that had no traffic with daylight, the drift of owls, endearing play of flying squirrels, untiring journey of the bats, fantastic commotion of a whippoorwill in the grass or bushes where you'll never find him.

Before too long Ethan arrived at another east-west highway that swept over hill and hollow as though the men of old time had cared nothing at all for the shape of the earth. Awe-struck and curious, he was nevertheless not inclined to follow it toward the sundown or sunrise. He still liked to hold the blaze of morning at his right hand. He chose a modest road that gave him this, and came at length, on a red evening, to a lake that spread serenely into the horizon.

This was a place for lonely thinking. Lazily, through several days, he made the circuit of the lake and settled in a place where the wild red raspberries delighted him. They were gone; it became July. Nothing human disturbed him here, nor any other dangerous animal.

About fifteen years before, a fire had swept the borders of the lake, removing whatever old signs of human intervention might have remained; second-growth pine, birch, poplar, hemlock and maple had healed and hidden the scars. The only paths now were trails the wild things made coming to drink at the water's edge. Ethan made none himself, gliding through the shadows softly as a panther, observing, killing as always only for food, occasionally sitting motionless for an hour in a state that he himself called "thinking with his muscles." He heard at such times no sound but bird song and insect stridency and wilderness cries; splash of fish jumping, beat of the lake's wind-ripples in the reeds; music of a storm, and of gentler winds that could start a hissing murmur in the pines. There would seldom be any creak of boughs, for all the trees were young here; the heavy-limbed giants had fallen in another age.

Ethan fished, and took the necessary game, and lived through pleasant untroubled hours, and discovered no words that would tell a woman what is love.

And no other clarifying thoughts would come to him. He dozed a good deal in this passive existence, sometimes even while he was watching the tall blue herons at work or the passage of white-headed eagles against the blue sky or the gray. He heard the resonant foolishness of loons across the lake in the evenings, and at night the hollow shouting of horned owls; he watched the patterns drawn on dim sky by the bats until he fell asleep. In this place he never saw the track of wolf or wild dog. Once or twice he fell into the notion that this might be a place God had set apart for lonely thinking, and he had entered it unworthily because just too damn stupid. Each time this thought sniggered at him he was able to dismiss it with derisive amusement, but it remained a trouble.

And then the very tranquillity of the region became a trouble, although he loved the lake no less. He found it difficult to recall the numbers and names of the days. This was serious: he must not lose track of the first of October. He pulled himself out of lethargy. He abandoned the lovely water to the sultry calm of August and journeyed on north toward a blue and silver and violet of mountains.

They had been waiting for him all the time. He had glimpsed them on clear days during his too great comfort at the lake. Now as his journey brought him near their foothills, it seemed to Ethan that if there were gods they must dwell in the serenity of these hills, these and no others. Real gods. Not the big blurry Something-There which was the best you could get out of the religious people at Shelter Town, but knowledgeable, easy gods, with the potential of kindness and cruelty—makers of storm and spring and winter and the green of wet poplar bark.

The educated people (like Claudius, who was certainly the best of them for all his crankiness and crazy notions), with their talk about the mighty proportions of the earth that made your own homeland a nothing, a speck of dirt—well, all right, but how did they know? In practice you had to face the world on the terms it gave you. Your touch was limited by the grasp of your hand or at most the flight of an arrow or a stone. You must see with the fleshly eyes in your own head; how could you trust the seeing that came through the difficult language of someone else (who might in spite of all his assurance be mistaken)?

It had been Ethan's habit to shrug and accept the sensible instruction of older people in Shelter Town: mountains are just elevations of the land surface; God is something larger than the Earth whom you pray to on Sundays, always being careful to think of him with capital letters (Him, Ethan!) and never letting Him become tiresomely definite. But now the big red-bearded man was growing increasingly convinced that up yonder among the summits of these mountains there might well be gods you could understand. Who might be reached, if they chose to permit it. Who might answer tough questions, if a man had the courage to ask them.

Why else should the great hills exist at all if not for beings nobler than men? Some half-felt absurdity in his logic bothered Ethan here; his mind closed it away and moved on, unaided by the thought that perhaps there could be more than one kind of truth.

You would not pray to such gods. Ethan had always felt at best childish, at worst idiotic, when going through the motions of prayer that Shelter Town considered advisable. It was pouring a make-believe passion into the wind. These gods who might be dwelling in the mountains—well, you would try to search them out, and face them, and (if they would allow it) speak.

He imagined asking them—in his fancy there was always a benign quiet about them; nothing ruffled them—what he might do with the strength that sometimes burned in him like pain, that ached after mighty consummations he had never found in toil, or women, or drink, or the methodical, unhating cruelty of hunting.

He might ask them: What is love?

And why such beings as Caleb were born.

And why Big Joe, who was probably his father, had to die drunk in the idiot foulness of a pack of hunting dogs.

It began to seem to him that he had always believed in these gods, or at least ever since glimpsing a triangle of silvered blue back there in his laziness at the lake and understanding what it might be. He regretted having lost so much time in those drowsy days, but maybe it didn't matter; maybe the gods had sent him a drowsiness because they were not ready for him to come to them. He was going to them now, and cheerfully, north by northeast. The morning was a promise in his right hand, spent by his left in the prodigal ripeness of evening. And he could see that there were mountains also to the west of him; but if any gods were dwelling over there, they should be the green simpler deities of the wilderness, who doubtless already knew him well enough but had no message that he needed.

He was following a road that aimed itself for the white hills, drawing him on to higher and higher ground. A moment came—it was a long day of heat and threatening storm—when he discovered that the peaks surrounded him everywhere except at his left, inaccessible yet seeming close. He could imagine the mountains themselves had moved a little to acknowledge his existence, he the small, impudent walking thing, the bug absurdly brave.

Could the men of the old time have built this road intending it to be a pathway to the gods? In spite of what was said in Shelter Town (and not denied by Claudius) about the shallowness of twentieth-century religion, the worship of trade, lust, comfort, money? Why else would those lost people have wanted a road leading up into the windy heights?

Ethan was startled by hoofprints appearing in the soft earth beside the road's blacktop. They came to it from a dim wood road at his right, and there were enough of them, both fresh and old, to suggest that the route was in regular use. There was horse dung, mostly dried out, but in one place it was fresh, and some of the hoofprints, all pointing up the road in the direction Ethan was taking, must have been made that day, perhaps only a few hours ago.

Ethan knew he could not have missed similar signs below that junction with the wood road. Bemused though he was by the mountains and the thought of the gods, and by a thousand unfamiliar journeyings of his thought, he was still too good a tracker and woodsman to miss anything like that. These horses had riders, or there would not be this definite, repeatedly traveled route; wild horses would have left their sign all over the mountainside. Some settlement had to be close by—down that wood road or up along the route he followed, or in both places. He walked on slowly, alert now and ready and worried, with skin-crawling uncertainty and a need to know.

For weeks now he had been giving scant thought to the people of his own breed, except for Eve Newman and her mother, and Claudius, who was illuminated in his memory by a devotion that had not significantly changed (jealousy of Claudius was just a joke, wasn't it?), and Kenneth Bellamy, who, blast him, always had good luck with women. Tightened up by the probable nearness of strangers, he contrived to make himself a stalking machine, not quite forgetting the gods but putting aside speculation because of the distraction it forces on a man; putting aside the bewilderments of love and any too great joy in the grandeur of the enlarging hills. It did occur to him, though, that if the gods did live in this airy region they surely had no reason to be angry with him and might even lend a hand if he fell into trouble, say, with members of his own species.

In this mood he was caught by certain residents of the Hampshire Grants, including the Governor.

It happened where the road crawled squirming along the shoulder of a cliff. Ethan had known some of the risks, not least of them a rising impetuous wind that was driving into the mountains from the southwest, confusing other sounds or overwhelming them. But the cliff was too steep to be scaled, and the drop of the slope below the road was nearly as bad. He had to follow the road itself or turn back, and Ethan would not turn back. He walked close to the blacktop's inner edge, studying the tracks that showed only occasionally on the loose shale and gravel which here took the place of earth along the shoulder. The horses, he had noticed, must be lighter than those that dragged the plows and wagons of Shelter Town; one was larger than the rest and made a deeper imprint, perhaps burdened by a massive rider.

Ethan kept glancing ahead at each new curve. It was no lack of common caution or good sense that betrayed him. While the wind swelled to a louder passion at his back and ears, the horsemen jingled around the bend up there, and with hardly a pause two of them, a thinly smiling youth and an old-faced man, pinned him with the threat of javelins against the wall of the cliff. The heavy black-bearded man on the red stallion said, "Well, what've we got here? Don't hurt him, boys. We got to find out things. Keep him nice and easy, just about like that." The boy's javelin hung an easy distance from Ethan's middle; the boy's face had the sweet-sickly, poisonous quality of one who has found pleasure in cruelty and boredom in everything else. The black-bearded man's voice was strong but with the suggestion of a whine, as though he were carrying on some unappeasable quarrel with himself; it suggested now: "Take his knife, Baldy. Baby's got him pretty well lined up. Just lift his knife and we'll have a little talk with him."

The older man dismounted and held out his hand for Ethan's knife. He had haunted, intelligent eyes; he was anywhere between forty and sixty, his scraggy beard iron gray. His shiny top wore no protection against sun and wind. If there was a message in his face for Ethan at all, it seemed to convey that he himself was no enemy, that Ethan would do well to play along and not get hurt. At his belt hung a revolver of the old time, a thing known in Shelter Town, its possession forbidden by law. Ethan gave up his hunting knife, mainly because of that quality in Baby's face. Baby wanted to kill something.

"All right," said the black-bearded man, "put up your pigsticker, Baby. Keep it handy, of course, but I think he's going to be nice. Where you from, Red?"

"South."

"You say 'Governor' when you speak to me, Red. Want you to remember that. You've come into the Hampshire Grants, and what we got up here is law and order is what we got. Want you to learn that right away. Fact is I could show you. Fact is we just did hang a man, up the road a piece. Maybe we'll take you up for a look at that after while."

"Hang?"

"Christ, don't they hang people where you come from?"

"I never heard of it," said Ethan.

Baby snickered. He had stepped his horse back a few paces without relaxing his vigilance. Toadying a little perhaps, Baby said, "Never heard of it, Governor."

"Well, like this," said the Governor. "Like this, Red. You stand a man up on something, say a barrel or a handy rock, with a rope around his neck and the other end of it fastened to a good high branch, and then you kick this barrel or whatever out from under him, after while he's dead."

"What for?"

Baby snickered again, but Baldy was only watching Ethan with his sober quiet.

"Why, in this case," said the Governor's rambling, excited whine, "in this case it was for plotting against the duly elected Governor of the Hampshire Grants. He was plotting overthrow of law and order was what he was plotting, didn't know my voices was sure to tell me. It's happened to better men than him—ha'n't it, Baldy?" He waited for no answer, but smiled thinly down at Ethan with the sickness of distrust. "God damn this wind! Red, you tell us right off and save a lot of trouble: what's your connection with Adrian Goldfarb?"

"I never knew anyone of that name. There was an Aaron Gold in the town I come from, died a couple of years ago."

"Well," said the Governor, "anyhow you admit you come from some God-damn place that's lousy with Jews, I guess that makes you honest or something. We'll pass it for the moment, about Goldfarb, except that's him up the road, that's Goldfarb we just got done hanging. What d' y' say, Baby? Did that make him jump a mite?"

Baldy said quickly, "He didn't jump, Governor. I'm standing here right next him. He didn't jump."

The Governor thought that over. Then as though his mind could not long focus on any one thing but must reach at random after bright fragments, he said, "Like my stud, Red?"

Ethan nodded. "He's a beauty."

The Governor reined in the stallion brutally, making

him dance. "Minds me, too. Knows who's Governor. What's the matter, Red—you a bleeding-heart? You don't look it." Ethan watched the javelin, the extension of Baby's arm, and did not speak. "Red, I could almost think you was my kind of man. Never figured you for a bleeding-heart. What's your name?"

"Ethan Nye is my name. I never took a fall from anyone."

"Why, Red! Anybody touched you? God damn this wind! Man can't hear himself think. Well, understand, Red, I'm kingpin in this country, which is the Hampshire Grants as far as the eye can see. You know what, Red? The human eye, this here human eye, I mean mine, keeps moving along and seeing further wherever I go. So any place I be, why, that's the Hampshire Grants. You start seeing it that way, it'll give you some idea who I am. You know any history, Red?"

"Some."

"Wha'd you say your name was?"

"Ethan Nye."

"E-thun—I should remember a noise like that? Never heard of any such name. E-thun. Red will have to do."

"I heard about an Ethan Allen in old time, Governor. He was historical as all hell."

"That's right, Governor," said Baldy and waved his arm to the west. "He lived over there a piece."

The Governor laughed, at some flurry in the confused country of his mind. "Bugger old time," he said. "This here is the progressive here and now is what it is. I may not look it, but I'm a self-made historical scholar and not ashamed of it. Damn near fifty though I don't look it, they tell me, and I went through high school, by God and by Jesus. Look, you think there's anything undemocratical about being a scholar? Well, these was the Hampshire Grants long ago. I read it in a book—I guess that takes care of people like Goldfarb that claim I can't read—and the Hampshire Grants is what they be now. Because I say so. Because it shows I got the *grant,* see, from God Almighty and the duly constituted democratical vote, to take care of law and order and the prustine virtues of the revolutionary spirit. And understand, Red, this ain't in just one pisswilly village that owes me 'legiance but all the way from the North Pole to the shores of the Atalantic, which I happen to know is somewhere south of here. You know about the prustine virtues, Red? Which is Number One?"

Without thinking—or perhaps he held some troubled thought that if the gods lived in these mountains they could be listening for his answer—Ethan said, "Honesty."

"A schoolboy's answer," said the Governor. "Politician's answer, except I can see you don't know nothing about politics. I been through all that myself. Done everything, except I guess kiss babies, had to draw the line at them little snots—hey, Baldy? Red, you listen to me—"

"Governor," said Baldy, "I just remembered something."

"What? What? I don't like the look on your face, Baldy." The black-bearded man seemed confused again, as if his attention were divided many ways.

"I'm all right," Baldy said. "I'll take care of my own face."

"You—you going back on me, Baldy? You?" The Governor appeared more frightened than angry, but then turned his gaze back to Ethan, manhandling the stallion with stiff hands on the reins. "I want you should understand about them prustine virtues, Red. You listen: obedience to the Governor of the Hampshire Grants—Governor Elihu Talbot, and that's me—is Number One. You get that into your head. And right now you can start telling me—God damn this wind!—telling me about this town you come from. No lies. Facts is what I want, facts."

Some involuntary noise happened in Ethan's throat. Baby exclaimed, "You laughing at the Governor? You—"

What followed was too rapid for Ethan's eye. There was the slam of Baldy's old gun, and Baby screamed. Baby's javelin clattered away somewhere, and Baby was staring at a reddening hole in his bare right arm. Unexcitedly Baldy explained, "He was about to gut you, Mr. Nye. Five-six years this ain't been fired, and I can still do it—ain't that a thing? Governor, you can send Baby home now. He's hurting, and no good to you or anybody, if he ever was. Not even to his Ma," said Baldy, looking again at Ethan and speaking with a calm note of explanation, "being she died a couple-three years back still possessed of the notion she could build him into something human."

Governor Talbot found his voice, a harsh and feeble thing. "You can't do this to me, Baldy. You been my good right hand. I trusted you when everybody else was conspiring to do me dirt. Like we'd growed up together, almost."

"I know, Elihu. It's like this stranger opened my eyes, some. Baby, you get. The grownups want to talk. You can manage them reins with your left. Get."

Whimpering with pain, not waiting for the Governor's word, the boy rode away. Talbot spoke more steadily: "What's come over you, Baldy?"

"Goldfarb never touched her."

"What? What?" They might have forgotten Ethan's presence. "You know he was guilty as hell. Man begins to conspire against the state, all the rest of his mor'ls go down the drain, if he ever had any—not that Goldfarb ever did, the son of a bitch."

"It was the rape and the killing that made me go along with you on the hanging, Elihu. Now I'm as guilty as you be, account of you and your voices had me that betwattled—God, I don't know. It wasn't Goldfarb. He was full of talk, maybe, but wouldn't hurt a bug. No, sir. You was whoring after her yourself. I can see it now— little things sort of fit together. You was after her yourself, and you come on her there in Parker's back field—"

"No, John, no!" The Governor dismounted, clumsily gripping the reins, and made as if to approach Baldy in some pleading way, but Baldy lifted the gun to keep him back. "Ah, John, you can't use that thing on me."

"Maybe I couldn't but don't come any closer."

Unaware that he was going to speak until it was too late to check himself, Ethan said, "Do the gods live in this place?"

Governor Talbot was staring at him. "The man's crazy." But Baldy was watching the Governor, holding his horse's reins, the stubby gun waiting in his other hand. The Governor walked his red stallion to the edge of the road and flipped the reins over his head. The horse stood, quivering, leashed lightning. Governor Talbot left him there and walked slowly toward the gun. "Baldy—Baldy- John—we can't have this. We been friends. Ain't we? Always?" Then he was near enough for a reckless grab at Baldy's wrist, and had it, forced it away to the side, and had old Baldy down, beating his head against the road. Baldy's frightened horse shied back away from the struggle.

The stallion held to his training, angry and scared but unmoving.

Ethan shrugged off his bow and quiver and shirt. Leaning down over Governor Talbot's laughing and writhing bulk, he pulled the Governor's knife and tossed it away. Then he hauled at Talbot's shoulder, wrenching him clear. As Talbot roared and closed with him, he was aware of Baldy crawling away.

Ethan had been unprepared for the older man's speed as well as his strength. They rolled over the blacktop like crazed tomcats. Ethan could no longer feel the wind but knew that it was blowing with unaltered fury, indifferent, and his mind was aware of the rim of the road as if it were a cave mouth, a vacuum pulling at him with the force of all the winds of the world. He had seen how the earth crumbled away from that rim, nothing visible below but an ugly slant of gravelly earth with here and there a twist of weak vegetation; it might be only a precarious heap of loose material between sections of the cliff.

Talbot's weight squirmed over him. The face above him was grinning with stupid blankness, or sadness. Ethan used all his power to bring up the heel of his hand against Talbot's jaw in its thick black shag of beard. The man was hurt a little. Blood appeared on his mouth from a bitten tongue; Talbot's momentary shock allowed Ethan to twist free and rise and step back. With the corner of his eye he saw that Baldy-John was holding both the horses, not much hurt, not showing much excitement. Waiting, perhaps, in his curious way.

Talbot was coming up into a crouch. They had been at the very edge of the road and might have gone over it. A rush at this instant, or a kick, might send the Governor into the abyss before he won back his balance. And Ethan could not do it—dazed himself, or unwilling the struggle should end that way, unwilling that the mountain of the gods should do his work for him. In a crowded instant of thought, while his enemy was recovering, it seemed to Ethan that he knew this man—knew him too well. He could predict Talbot, feel with him. There was a spreading horror in the truth of it. He knew Talbot as if the man were his twin brother; in Talbot there would be that same goading blind energy that became agony if thwarted. He watched Talbot blinking, gulping in air, loins quivering in readiness for the next rush, and he

thought: *What happens to a man who kills his brother?*
*God damn this wind! If the gods live here, can't they stop
what will happen?* Then Talbot was coming for him in a
rush. Ethan met him with a braced hip, and spilled him,
and held him pinned.

The mad purpled face glared up at him and changed,
fading to sudden whiteness, slackness, emptiness. Ethan
said, "Is it enough, then?" The open eyes no longer ac-
knowledged him; the sagging mouth, still bloody from a
bitten tongue, had no words. Ethan said, "But—but he
wasn't hurt much."

"Heart maybe," said Baldy laconically. "I believe you
had it to do. Know anything about horses? Come take
the stud, boy. He's nerved up and won't stand much
longer without a real hand onto him, better than mine."

Ethan took the stallion's bridle. He loosened the bit
and gentled the horse with a hand grown hungry for acts
of kindness. "You grew up in the old time, didn't you?"

"Sixty-two, unless I lost a year or two some place. Mr.
Nye, will it be all right with you if I send his body over
the edge? See, the Presidential Range, it ain't no burial
ground, only in the valleys. If there's any deep earth up
here the tree roots have it and welcome. Up here the old
earth's bone is close to the skin—that's how it is. Will I
do that, Mr. Nye?"

"I don't know. Yes—yes, do that. I came here thinking
—I came here—" but Baldy was moving away for his
brief task, and Ethan petted the stallion's neck and tried
to stop his sudden childish weeping. *What is love?* He
saw Talbot's body was gone, and Baldy with his handsome brown horse, somewhere over there, not too far away.
"I came here thinking the gods lived in the hills. Now
I've got death on my hands, I that never hurt anyone! It's
too much," Ethan raged. "How am I supposed to carry
what I am?"

"Why, Jesus, boy, you had it to do, I think. You got
him off me, or I'd be dead as Goldfarb. Then he rushed
you, what the hell."

"It's not that. Don't you see? I . . ." But he could not
find any words. "What's your name, your real name?"

"Been called Baldy a long time."

"But your real name?"

"John Chilton. Good name too. *Mayflower* name if
that means anything to you, Mr. Nye. Know what this

man was Governor of? Seven families. The village is the other side the ridge down yonder—wood road goes to it, likely you saw it. Lebanon. Seven families. Mostly old folks and beat out, but a few young ones coming along. Mighty few. That's one reason why when little Joan Messenger got abused and strangled, why, well, all of us went sort of out of our heads. Only it couldn't've been Goldfarb. Easy enough to see it now when it's too late. He couldn't've hurt a fly on the wall. Uh-huh, mostly old folks, but still farming it, or trying to, on the upended flat side of nothing, way they always did in these parts. Come from Connecticut myself, so they still call me a foreigner, been here only thirty-six years. Can't blame 'em for that. It's natural. Him and his Hampshire Grants."

"What's up ahead?"

"Goldfarb."

"I meant—along the road. Where does the road go?"

"Summit. About Governor Talbot, you should know he was a lot of man at one time. See, he took over when things went to hell in a bucket—I mean the war, the sicknesses, all that. I can see you're too young to've lived through it. Talbot, he was . . . manager, sort of. He held us together, kept things in order, lent a hand to anyone that needed it. Big, noisy, kind of ignorant, but a useful man. A good man. More and more we got to doing whatever he said. Got to be a habit—except with Adrian Goldfarb, who was a-mind to do things his own way, and one or two others, but there never was an ounce of harm in Adrian. God, I dunno when it was things began to go wrong with Elihu Talbot. You couldn't say any special time. Might be it was when somebody called him 'Governor' like for a joke and he took it serious. All that power in him, straining with no place to go."

"I know," said Ethan.

"Nah, you're all right, boy. I know people. I been around some. Don't fret so about yourself. You'll do to go on with. But old Elihu, I guess he had to be king, no matter if there wasn't nothing to be king of no more. And he had this way with him—you know? At his best he could charm the brass knocker off a door, and maybe that's why little Joan hadn't sense enough to run. God damn his sick old soul, I guess I'll always believe he done it."

"In spite of himself maybe?" Ethan asked. "In spite of himself?"

"I don't know, and no more could you. Well, you take me—I been going around with old Elihu years, yessing him, partly believing I could stop the worst of his notions when things come to a head. But I seen him do some pretty bad things in the past, Mr. Nye, and it'd always be the *next* time I was going to do something. And his charm, his God-damn charm. He had me honestly believing it about Goldfarb—just long enough."

It came to Ethan that Claudius Gardiner had said once, "Uncertainty is only one of the basic conditions of life." Maybe, Ethan thought, he could begin to understand that now, if he could get away from this trouble here on the road and his part in it, far enough away to think it out. "You said this road goes to the summit?"

"Uh-huh. Used to be a lookout, picnic place in the old days. They'd drive up in them old buzz-buggies we used to take for granted and look at the God-damn view."

Some versions of the legend leave out Baldy-John Chilton entirely. This is ridiculous: someone had to hold the horses, and besides, there *was* a Chilton on the *Mayflower* (who, if he'd taken his duties as an ancestor more seriously, would have tried to be less of a problem and more of a hot shot). The versions that snub Baldy-John are apt to be the same ones that begin: "There were once three heroes of Massachusetts"—which stamps them as arrant trash. There may be no certain proof that Kenneth Bellamy was originally from New Hampshire, but there is not a shadow of doubt that Claudius Gardiner was born in the state of Maine.

"Will you go up there with me, John Chilton?"

"Might as well. Take the stud."

Ethan recovered his gear; the stallion accepted him in gracious obedience. Ethan was remembering the stillness of his lake in the evening, and he wondered if this wind blew forever crying across the top of the world. They rode up the blacktop, past the cliff and out on the easier ground of a broad ridge. John Chilton said, "I'll stop here a minute. Go on, Mr. Nye, if you're a-mind—or help me cut him down, if you're a-mind. I don't want the old man swinging there. I can't see there was ever any harm in him."

"I'll help you," said Ethan; but he was not of much

help, for he was sickened by the congestion of the dead face, the grotesque unreason of the actions that, he was learning, men could carry out against each other. The stocks in Shelter Town were bad enough, but—as yet, so far, in Ethan's time—men had not dealt each other death. It was Baldy who carried the frail and ruined body off under a screen of trees.

"Some-way it's better," Baldy said, returning. "I can't think why. Ain't as if he cared. Some-way I didn't want him swinging there for the crows."

"I guess it's better," said Ethan, sick and scarcely hearing him. "Let's ride on."

"All right. Road ends at the summit, no place to go but back. If I was a younger man, Mr. Nye, I might be a-mind to go further with you than that—for I take it you're traveling, with some distance yet to go. But I ain't a younger man. Plan to stay with us in Lebanon for a spell?"

"I don't know. There's a woman waiting for me. I must be back with her when the leaves are coloring—in time to cut wood for the winter and such like."

"That's good," said Baldy, old and uninvolved and kind. "It's good you should have a woman waiting, Mr. Nye."

The stallion, growing familiar with his new rider in his own fashion, seemed undismayed by the wind but rolled a whitened eye at flashes of light in the darkened southwest. The light was blooming too far away for any noise of thunder to arrive here on the heights. When Ethan and his companion reached the summit the storm seemed to have drawn no nearer: one could think, if one was so inclined, of the unimaginable wars and fires of other ages.

The summit was only a place where one discovered other summits.

Ethan rode forward alone to the edge of the lookout, Baldy holding back among his own thoughts.

Eastward and southward was infinity; in the west, infinity and storm. To the north, Ethan saw the masses of greater hills dwarfing the one where he could climb no higher. To the northwest stretched a long granite ridge, part of his own mountain but at least half a mile away from him across a gap filled with the toy tops of trees. Something was moving over there.

He watched it, friendly and curious. The long cat body

seemed too massive in proportion to the legs to be right for a panther; even at that distance that and other differences were apparent to his hunter's eye. Well, it would be natural if these hills were inhabited by creatures unknown elsewhere, and never mind about the gods. Maybe some time he would come back here to hunt and learn a little.

The tiger paused on that ridge, silhouetted against the cool light of the north, so that Ethan could not be sure whether or not it stared toward him. Nor does the legend say.

The stallion neighed at the world below him, and Ethan laughed and shouted, forgetting Baldy-John Chilton, forgetting his sickness: "Are you here?" He listened, hearing only the wind. More quietly he said, "I am here." And then after a while, not in impatience, he called, "John Chilton—here's a curious thing. I came up here believing it might be where the gods live."

John Chilton rode to him then across the old lookout place and cupped a hand at his ear against the wind. Ethan repeated the words, but the old man only smiled in noncommittal kindness and let his hand drop, looking westward with nothing to tell concerning the gods out of the meditations of his own age.

PART THREE

The Judgment of Eve

1. The Welcome

The evening bore the chill of the advancing season. In Caleb it stirred a shapeless recollection of other times when warmth faded from the earth, the forest abandoned green to a bewilderment of bright colors and then lost them too, and there were nagging rains, the wind could be a whip, and presently there came severe whiteness and the new stillness.

He brought the sheep into the fold for safety. The ram was restless with premonitions of rut. Ordinarily Caleb would have remained to watch him, moved to curiosity and dull excitement, but this year nothing was the same as it had been in other days. He slipped through the barn and rounded the house and took up his post on the top of the old tilted bus, lonely, listening, waiting.

He had been doing that all summer long, as soon as his day's work was done—in the middle daytime too, if Eve released him from his toil in the garden or woodlot or hayfield. Often she did.

Eve was gentler with him than in other summers. Mama was the same; Mama never changed. But this year Eve's voice seldom took on the edge of anger. When he blundered she was more likely to laugh than scold. Unable to make any true comparison with earlier times, Caleb did know that his work was light these days, his existence easy, his punishments rare. Mama never whipped him any more. When Eve did it, Eve's hand was light—the meaning was clear, the pain almost nothing.

Caleb noticed, puzzled afresh whenever it happened and then forgetting it, that when he needed guidance and sought to attract Eve's attention, it might be difficult to rouse her from her own lazy stillness. She could look straight at him with a frightening lack of focus, a not-there appearance, before the blue-green eyes cleared and her natural self took over.

And Caleb remembered the tall man who had gone away. He had no idea how long the tall man might have been present. One evening and morning of adoration were in his mind large as a year.

When the three were taking their leave, Caleb had heard several times the words "come back." Mama herself had spoken them, and the men, and Eve. Imperfectly the speech-noise connected with certain familiar words of command, so that some of the true meaning of the farewell conversation came through to him. And then down on the hillside road the tall god-man had repeated the words—before he got angry (while the red hairy one laughed and the little one just stood there) and made it clear that Caleb could not follow him. Some of the pain of that incident lingered in Caleb like a lamed muscle.

Come-back—it was a blur, yet even with the summer gone some of its power remained. Caleb felt it most strongly during these hours of watchfulness on top of the bus, with no need to explain to himself just why he should be here at this time. The hours might stretch on well into the night, especially under a clear moon. He needed little sleep.

He crouched on the slanting metal roof, a part of the dark, and shivered at the wind that carried in it the death of September, but would not give up the vigil early. Giving it up meant shambling off to his pallet by the kitchen door—pleasant warmth and smells and nearness of the familiar Rulers—but he wasn't ready for that. He would wait for the white light.

It came, slow in the east, an hour after dark was complete. Caleb stood up then, weary and drowsy but persistent, braving the mean sharpness of the wind until the full moon had gone through its change from red to gold to burning silver.

Nothing to see in the region of the road. Nothing to hear except the wind's whine and thrust, scratch of a flying dead leaf across his chest. He moaned and mumbled and rubbed an itch on his belly, jumped down at last and trotted to the rope at the loft window. Up then, and down, and through the barn to flop on his pallet with a gross thud and animal squirmings. Warmth and smells were good, and they swallowed his spirit. He grumbled and whimpered his way into sleep, and whatever dreams he encountered there would be unique, altogether distinct from all other dreams ever experienced by animal or man, like yours, and would remain forever inaccessible, untransmitted, lost on waking to Caleb himself. Those later-century tellers of the legend of the Judgment of Eve may have been aware of Caleb's dreams, but never mentioned them. One tidies up after them a little: a bit of exegesis here and there, another chipped flint on top of a pyramid which can readily bear the weight.

"I thought," said Alma Newman, "that I'd have no trouble keeping track of the days. I never did before. You haven't spoken of the calendar today, so it must be near the last day of September."

"The last day, Mama."

What was that in the voice from the other side of the fireplace? Joy? Some, probably. Fear? Maybe. Uncertainty, of course. And what if no one came tomorrow? The old woman shrank at thought of Eve's imagined pain, and tried to dismiss the weakness—the tiger of Claudius Gardiner's note must be walking on her grave.

Nothing, she knew, except a myriad ordinary contacts over the years, could prepare a human being for the disappointments that others continually provide. Children never expect them; for a child, each new betrayal or apparent betrayal is a fresh outrageous wound. Then in time there's enough callus and scar tissue so that the grownup can elbow alone on his own journey—or there isn't, maybe, and he lives wincing, retreating, hiding in deeper and deeper burrows until it's time for the Fool-killer to root him out. Alma Newman said, "Dear, I'm wondering—it must be difficult for anyone traveling around the country the way it is now to keep track of the calendar. You'd need to make one, I should think, and be careful to cross off each day, or cut notches in a stick, something like that. Then there'd come the one time when you'd forget to cut your notch, or couldn't recall for sure whether you'd done it, and so confusion—like what I had just now. In the old days we had the very present time thrust at us continually—newspaper date lines, a calendar in every kitchen or living room, rhythm of workdays and weekends."

"They won't forget," said Eve, and in the voice then there was a living music of confidence—confidence in the men at least, whether or not she felt it in herself. "I'm going to set candles in some of the windows upstairs. Well, it's got dark enough. I think I'll do that right now." And from the doorway the girl spoke more slowly and thoughtfully: "Not that I expect them until tomorrow—

maybe not even then, if they lose track, as you say—but I wouldn't want them to come and find no light." Alma Newman heard her go upstairs—not running but slowly, almost heavily, and in the suddenly cooler room she found no hiding place.

What if one, or two, came, but not the one, whichever it was, that Eve desired?

If no one came—well, unshielded by experience against any such hurt, she would begin dying. And her own mother might not quite know it immediately, might have no clue to subtle changes in the girl's voice as she ceased to be a girl or anything like a girl: the sounds of hope against despair, then hope against reason, and in time perhaps despair without reason—apathy, ruin of youth, loneliness becoming a sickness of the mind.

They would have to take to the road. But how? Winter was on the way now. *Retreating again, Mrs. Newman?* Almost prosaically, she wondered whether she ought not to die. *But don't think it, or you'll be saying it to Eve!* She hadn't said it already, had she? No: what she remembered was the sound of her own mother's voice, saying that. Not much help, the blue satin pillows, day and night nurses, Park Avenue doctor and Daddy's forty thousand a year—all froth when the cancer took hold and morphine ceased to be enough. It must have been something the other side of hell, surely, or she wouldn't have made that speech to a child whenever the child dutifully appeared.

And could only dread and half hate the sick woman for the sound of it. I'm sorry, Mother. And for the smell that relentlessly came through the smells of perfumes and medications. Like a tiger behind bars, but the bars are only smoke.

And when did being sorry ever matter? The mud old words we use! I'm sorry, Mother.

"Mama, what is it? What is it?"

She had not heard Eve returning. "Oh, tears are—I remember reading old people don't always have good control—it's a muscle weakness or something. I think there was a puff of smoke from the fireplace, the wind's in such an autumn passion. See if the logs need pushing back. Be truthful, Eve—honestly, didn't you like one of them just a slight bit more than the others? Come now!"

"I'd tell you if I was sure at all. We've talked at it and all around it, all summer, haven't we? Ah, maybe there was a—a kind of preference. But when I see them again maybe it'll be gone, or changed, and then I'd feel such a fool. But what about you—wasn't there one you liked best? Claudius maybe?"

"Oh, simply because he belonged to my time—and of course you don't get to be the kind of interpretive artist he was without what we used to call strength of character. No, Eve, I liked all three, and more I won't say—except that we were most fortunate, considering the kind of horrible creatures that might have descended on us any time these twenty-five years. I won't say more—the boys aren't courting *me*, darling. It seemed to me I felt kindness and honor in all three. Honor—how desperately unfashionable that word was in my time! Can you imagine people being actually ashamed of honor, honesty, goodness, kindness? Well, they were—half a century of imperfectly digested psychology, I guess—one of the things that may have prepared the disaster. What was I saying? Oh, and it seemed to me those three all possessed courage of different kinds. Like people anywhere, any time, they naturally weren't carrying their faults in plain sight. I felt as much kindness in your Bear-Strangler as in the rest, by the way—maybe more."

"Don't call him that, Mama! He didn't like being laughed at. Call him Ethan. And he's not mine unless I say so, as I haven't."

"Cross, ain't she! A man's got to learn how to stay cool when he's laughed at. He'd better; the world does it all the time. And especially when he's laughed at by women. Watch how a man takes that type of gunfire and you learn a lot about him, Eve. Laughter of other men and strangers —different, just as important, I guess—he must bear that too. I'd rate Ethan pretty well on both counts. Bellamy— it could be, dear, that Kenneth Bellamy hasn't been laughed at quite as much as he needs, nor taken seriously as much as he needs."

"And Claudius?"

"Oh, a man of his age has got used to the crackling of thorns and the belly-roaring of the gods long ago or else died inside, and Claudius hasn't died inside, not yet. I think I want to turn in, darling, though it's early. Nobody's coming till daylight, but you do promise to wake me if you hear anything?"

"Of course, Mama."

"I'm just tired—'my old brain is troubled: be not disturbed with my infirmity—' "

"You're stealing Prospero's lines. Act Four, Scene One. Comes at the end of the big one with the cloud-capp'd towers."

"Well, I've had to be father and mother. And have given you some education, I believe?"

"Whatever I am—"

"Dear, just help me up to bed."

After her mother had fallen asleep Eve visited the candles she had placed in the upper windows. One she blew out because it was flickering too much in a draft caused by the boisterous shoving and threatening of the west wind. This was a window at the rear of the house, in a small room her mother had liked to use for sewing before her eyes failed. No one would be coming from that direction surely. Eve stood in the chilly dark gazing up at the scarcely visible bulk of Wake Hill, and shivered, not from cold but from awareness of the west wind's wrath. Nothing to hold away the assault but a frail shield of glass, transparent, a membrane of nothing. *How did we make glass in the days when we could make things? We, I said. And ah, ah, says the wind, a penny for them, Miss Newman? Oh, just wondering, as I have a perfect right to do, about the breaking of glass and other tender things.*

Her mother's self of ten, fifteen, even twenty years past came near to her in this little room, so familiar that darkness made it only more eloquent. Alma Newman had made it a refuge as well as a work place. Even this last summer she had sometimes groped her way to it, not wanting to be guided, and had sat in tranquillity by the window where mild summer air could touch her blind face—and safe, Eve supposed, so long as she remembered she mustn't sit out alone in the sun. *And what is a tiger, really? The books and pictures—you can't think tiger, when even the timid tawny panthers have been no more than a glimpse. But you can think terror.* She relived some of the shock (and doubtful pleasure) of discovering Claudius' note on the side porch. *He was near, maybe even saw me find it.*

She had studied the brush fence, the distant edge of the woods, that morning and every morning since. No more comfortable loafing on that lookout rock in the upper pasture—which made her, for a while, unreasonably irritated not at the fact of tiger but at Claudius.

Escaping from the insolence, the rowdy persistence of the west wind, Eve stole downstairs and set a fresh log on the fire. Caleb might be asleep by the kitchen door, but she heard none of his usual grunts and fidgets. More likely keeping his pathetic vigil on top of the bus, and he might stay out there in the cold till the moon's rising. *Mooncalf —and how much better am I? Stupid brainy bitch, why would they ever come back to you? Why don't we go out together in the long grass, Caleb and I? Shall I flatten myself on all fours, Caleb, my little playmate? Poor fella, did he get whipped then?*

She was quiet, not in her usual place but in her mother's wing chair, sitting on her feet in the red-green dressing gown—careful of it, though—warm, crying for a time and then again motionless, and growing drowsy but not expecting nor desiring sleep. "Let us come back in time to cut wood for the winter."

The tall man came back for the scarf he meant to leave behind, and wonderful was the gray darkness of his eyes (though apparently they couldn't see too well) and more wonderful the sureness of his kiss that transmitted (and he knew it) a wordless electric message: *If I choose to take you, how in the world can you say no?*

Wonderful was the saucy blue keenness of other eyes (which saw extremely well) and the mildness that belonged with his impossible strength. *No, a man doesn't strangle a bear, but that fancy is for enjoyment and I am standing, say, over there, and when he's done it (which is extremely hard on the bear) and he turns to me, then I—well, I . . .*

Wonderful, those pain-and-thought wrinkles around his eyes (and they probably saw this world as any man's eyes should, but were bitter and without contradiction, compassionate from having seen too much in the world that died) and more wonderful the sense (he knew she felt it, didn't he?) that she might speak to him of anything at all (almost anything) and not be distrustful or ashamed.

"I'm simple," Ethan said. "Can't change myself much, Eve, and never was good with words. But I'll go look some more at what's out there and maybe find me some words for you after all."

He let the scarf drop to her hips a moment and pulled it to bind her against him and said, "You're beautiful, Eve. I love you."

He said: "We'll come back in time to cut wood for the

winter."

Maybe the makers of the original legend wanted to leave some freedom to later tellers of the story. Didn't Homer leave us free to imagine what occurred in the heart of Nausicaa? Eve lived, therefore she thought.

And yawned, and banked the fire carefully, and carried her candle upstairs, and spread another blanket over her mother's bed against the deepening frost of the night.

Then doubtfully she opened the door of the other bedroom, the one that her father and mother had used long ago, the one that her mother had suggested she might now prepare for other occupancy if she wished, if she thought best, if it turned out that way. Eve had started the little task, but timidly, not quite ready to allow such a wide-open invitation to disappointment. She had opened and aired the room, swept, dusted, hung fresh curtains; but the closet was empty and she had installed none of her small treasures; sheets and blankets lay still folded on the big bed. And now she glanced in just briefly, to make certain the candle she had set in the east window was safe and orderly, the curtains securely fastened back away from it. And having come in, she stepped to the window and saw the rising moon, and Caleb out there on top of the bus, looming in a somewhat brave imitation of the shape of a man.

Here on the lee side of the house the west wind allowed her to think of other night sounds. Somewhere in the moon-governed solitude—on Wake Hill, perhaps, or in the forgotten village—she heard a howling of wolves and understood she was not afraid.

She went back then to the small bedroom she and her mother had shared for the comfort of each other's presence since she was a child, and not expecting even to find rest, she slept.

Her mother roused her. Unwontedly sluggish as if the night had wearied her out, finding it hard to grope away from dissolving dreams, Eve knew the cock had been crowing in the barn for some time with his witless cheerful persistence, and the west wind was stilled. Only then did she understand her mother's voice, its urgency: "Eve! Wake up! I heard a horse neighing."

"A horse?" Something from the books. A beast of graceful lines and sentimental stories. Real too, of course. Now she was awake and saw the light had gone some way beyond dawn. She had not wanted to sleep late, certainly not on this day.

"Go look from the roadside windows, Eve. I know I didn't dream it—I was lying wide awake when the sound came. Oh, be careful! *Don't show* yourself at the window until you can see it's one of our friends. The rifle—you must have the rifle with you before you go to the window."

"It's all right, Mama. Everything under control, and here we go!"

The candle in the east bedroom flaunted a wisp of fire, wan in daylight. Heedless of her mother's warning, Eve stepped into the full light to blow it out and saw the red-bearded horseman standing in the early sunshine where once there had been a road. Heedless, flooded with pleasure, gratitude, love, friendship, Eve flung the window wide open and called to him, "Ethan! Good morning to you!"

He waved and grinned pridefully, wheeled his horse and ran him for the barrier of the brush fence, which the red stallion jumped with disdainful ease, never brushing a twig. Ethan was under the window, a smiling centaur. Sober and frightened and unsure but no less delighted with him for all that, Eve said in shyness, "I'll come down in a minute and let you in."

He dismounted and waited by the door. In a way it resembled a certain time of dazed apprehension long ago, ecstasy on the edge of sickness, when Big Joe Nye had pointed silently with eyes and chin toward dappled shadows that were becoming a deer, indicating that Ethan's bow should take it. Amused anger at himself simmered now behind his bearded face. *Look, Eth: you've known women, you've had 'em, and she's a woman. She's not about to broil you for her breakfast. Seems to me a man ain't captive unless he chooses.*

The worst she could do right now was of course fairly rough—making him wait another ten minutes or so while birdlike sounds went on within the house that might or might not concern him. Had she forgotten him? No doubt. Probably the others had already arrived, and the lot of them were stretching awake after a night of revelry and laughing at his lateness, his simple stupidity.

The stallion stood bravely, reins over his head. Baldy-John had told Ethan the stud would always do that—trained as a colt in a rather tough school. Ethan had learned a number of other things too from Baldy-John

Chilton and the people of Lebanon; still it seemed to him in retrospect that most of his time in the seven-family village had been devoted to arguments, especially about the calendar. By their reckoning it was three days earlier than by his, and with Eve on his mind he knew he couldn't be wrong; but they explained their views with a somber New England rightness that left Ethan helpless—after all, no man single-handed is going to circumcise the Empire State Building*—and he could only sputter that he wasn't going to go to church on Thursday and no town meeting would be low enough to make him.

There were other problems to create friction. When Ethan arrived the village was divided, and had been for a long time, on the question whether clam chowder should be made with or without tomato and/or potato. This had some of the desperate qualities of a border war, because of a fierce infiltration of New York opinion some thirty-five years back. In Lebanon's population of 29, including the children, the aged, and the infirm, feeling ran high— still does among their descendants, of course. Since Ethan had grown up guzzling clam chowder in coastal Shelter Town, and these good people were too far inland to have seen a clam for at least twenty-five years, it did seem to the red-bearded boy that he had some right to an opinion. He told them he liked it a mite better without either, but —tomato-potato-shmomato—he was damn-blasted if he didn't think it was pretty good any style so long as there was plenty of clam, with biscuits on the side and real food to follow. Clearly the fence-sitter has more chance than most of getting ridden on a rail. Since Ethan Nye was far too big and healthy for that, both factions took it out in special moments of freezing politeness whenever they heard the sound of some word resembling clam (damn, slam, ham, etc.) until the time came when he had to leave. Then the women cried and said he was cute, and several of the men appeared shyly with small presents that had a lot of heart behind them—a dog-eared *Farmer's Almanac,* for instance, and one of Cousin Amalthea's hand-painted oils with a weep-and-willow that was real lifelike except that little spot right there where Grandfather's left eye showed through some—never had liked that one of

*A twentieth-century tower of which many ancient photographs exist. The author doubtless means it was too big.

Grandfather, and Cousin Amalthea was perfectly right to paint over it, it done him justice but see, that was just what you didn't want, having him look like the miserable old skinflint son of a bitch that he was.

Eve opened the door. "My mother says it's a frightful hour to be calling on a lady, but I say it's—oh, Ethan!" Now he could look on her beauty deepened and sweetened by absence and the summer's passing, and he was rocked on his solid heels by her impulsive embrace. Holding her so—like a fawn, a fledgling—he forgot many of the other activities of youth, including amusement at his elders. But her face was down on his shirt. Except for a first friendly peck on the cheek she would not kiss him. In a moment she was saying, "Are the others with you, or coming soon?"

"I haven't seen them since we left that morning, Eve. We separated down in the old village."

"And then did you go traveling a long way, Ethan? Did you see a thousand places I've never heard of, and other people, and think a lot, and find out—find out—"

"Some other people, but no, I didn't go very far. I spent a good part of the time near a wonderful lake, by myself. I keep thinking how fine it would be to go there with you sometime, Eve, if . . ." But she wouldn't speak. "I stayed there a long time because—oh, it seemed to me I might travel all over the world and yet never know any more about what love is—if there really is any way of putting it into words—than I could learn by watching the sun come and make the day and die in the evening, there by that lake. And listening to the wind as if it was no more than my own self saying I love you."

He saw he might have kindled something in her. There was a glance of delight and kindness; perhaps it meant more than that. But she turned her face away so quickly he could read no more, only stare at the delicate veining of her eyelids, the pucker of a slight frown, the comic flirt of her tongue tip passing neat as a kitten's across the full upper lip. His hands dropped away from her. He asked, "Do you like the horse? His name is Star, I was told, and he seems to know it. Come talk to him."

"I never saw one before, only pictures. Isn't he wild, Ethan? He's so beautiful he must be wild, surely. Ah, Star! Wild?"

"There's wildness in him, but it won't turn against you

or me. Rub his neck a little. See? He quits that nonsense
about showing the whites of his eyes when you touch
him. He likes you. Eve—"

"Don't try too hard for words, Ethan, not for a while
anyway. Maybe I know more than you think without
needing any words."

"Well . . . You know, a man needs horses to make a
farm. I'm a hunter, always have been, but I've thought
I'd quit that and make a farm when I—well, got married.
This little stud, he's a Morgan, they told me—up at Lebanon, where I got him—and they said that's a breed
meant for saddle and carriage, but with work-horse mares
like some I know I could get at Shelter Town, why, he
could sire some fine colts. Then, see, with a work team—
well, for instance, you take that field off there back of the
barn, it must be good ground or it wouldn't grow that
kind of grass, early land too, the drainage must be good,
but you see how the brush and trees have been moving
in, they've stolen a lot from you already. Just this summer they've stolen a lot." He breathed deeply, loving her.
"Now with a work team we can . . . could push the woods
back, hold 'em back. I remember you said you kept some
wheat going, year to year—why, with a work team that
whole field there could go into wheat, maybe kind of a ro-
tation, buckwheat, I don't know, corn—wouldn't be too
much for one man with a work team. Give it a bit of
time, the fields could be expanded some, cut and cleared,
year or two afterward the horses could pull the stumps
pretty good. Takes time, of course, a little patience." *For
God's sake, Eth, can't you ease up on the noise? She keeps
listening and smiling, but—oh, the mother.*

"I'm glad you've come back, Ethan Nye." To his eyes
she appeared more old and frail, as if the summer had
taken much from her. Bent and white, with a tremor in
her left hand gripping the doorway that he could not remember noticing in May.

He said to Eve, "Just hold onto the bridle. He'll be-
have." He hurried to take hold of the old lady's right
hand, which came out to him as she smiled in his direction. In the summer he had nearly forgotten Mrs. Newman was blind. "I did mean to strangle a bear for you,
but they all ran too fast."

"Oh, I don't mind," she said. "I see in your travels
you've learned to talk some. I like that, Ethan. I'm very

pleased about that. So much of the world's hard work that can't be done without words—a shame, but that's how it is, I guess. By the way, we have a box stall in the barn where you could put up your horse—I think it's clear of junk. Dear Ethan, how I wish I could *see* him! I used to ride quite a bit when I was a young girl. What's his color?"

"Bright roan, I think they call it—red-roan."

"With white forefeet," said Eve. "And white on his head."

"That's his star," said Ethan. "I think a child with a bit of know-how could handle him, he's that clever. All right, I'll put him up out there if it's all right."

"Show him where, Eve. Isn't Caleb around?"

But, slouching out of the barn as Eve and Ethan approached it, Caleb cowered and shrank at sight and smell of the red stallion (and perhaps at Ethan too) and might have fled gibbering to the woods if Eve had not checked him with a peaceful word.

"Don't be afraid," said Ethan and offered Caleb his hand, and went on with the kind of soothing, questionless talk he might have used for gentling a worried animal, some creature with less brain than the red stallion and probably less heart. "I'm Ethan—you remember me. All I do is strangle bears. I'm all right. I'm only a little guy." Caleb reached timidly for his hand.

And Eve was watching.

But though Ethan felt he was acting a part under the observation of the blue-green eyes, he discovered no falsity in it. This morning, without thinking about it, he could include the idiot lump within that region called love whose boundaries are no more, no less constant than the boundaries of sunlight or grief or memory. Any living thing approaching Ethan at that moment would enter the region and be loved.

The unliving too. He loved the silvered shingles of the barn roof, the fading grass meeting October in the field beyond, the glowing descent of a leaf through morning air that carried almost no reminder of the night's west wind. Ethan looked with love at the pines bordering that field. A man with a good team would push them back about *so,* make the field near-about eight acres altogether, close as you could tell without pacing it off. He looked with love at Wake Hill, its gracious breastlike mound. Eve was saying, "Tell me more about the horse. Where did you find him? And this neat thing. Bridle? Halter? Oh!" Without waiting for an answer she was running away through the grass, laughing and calling out another name. Ethan could feel the stab of jealousy and yet immediately take within the reach of his love the gnarled man who had come out from among those pines and walked toward them through the field carrying an old-time weapon, a rifle no less, but laying it down before Eve reached him so that he could catch her up (with one arm!) and kiss her mouth.

"Every *day* all summer *long* there's been something or other I needed to ask you about that Mama couldn't answer and oh, not only about the old time, but—Claudius, what's been happening? Where did you go? How come the rifle? You didn't have one before, and of course that note about the tiger, we tried to—anyway you're safe and healthy, you look good. Oh, damn, I did miss you! And so where—"

He says in the *Notes* that although he believes she did cherish him as a fount of wisdom and information (and for other reasons) it was still ten minutes before he could get three consecutive words in by the thin edge. The statement is probably accurate if you knock, say, eight off the ten—always seems longer if your own talk-mill is loaded with something you think will sound bright. His obvious tenderness for her seems never to have obscured for Claudius the fact that Eve liked to talk even more than he did himself. By the time her first welcome for him had simmered down, the stallion was in the barn snorting discontentedly at the smell of sheep, and everyone else was in the kitchen, Eve back at work poaching eggs (no coffee; what a hell of an age!) and fretting in her heart about Kenneth Bellamy.

"Well, he went into Redfield with me. At the time we separated I think he was still intending to take the westward road out of the city. Before then we'd managed to find some glasses that corrected his nearsightedness pretty well. The wreck of an old store. I even found this pair for myself, seems to be a help in reading."

"Oh, good heavens!" said Eve from her work at the stove. "The owl of a man!"

"Uh-huh. Schwab's, optician."

"Why," said Alma Newman, "I remember Mr. Schwab. I got my last pair of glasses there—it must have been in

'70. We always had to go to Redfield for that kind of shopping. He had little blond sideburns and liked to tell me about his pigeons. He lived over the store and kept his homers or racers or whatever they were up on the roof. Didn't get on too well with his wife, could be the pigeons were a consolation."

"Pigeons don't seem to be around the city any more. Depended on human beings too much, perhaps. We saw an eagle's nest on the roof of the Eastern Life Insurance Building."

"Mm," said Alma Newman, far away.

Eve had optimistically killed two roasting chickens that day. There were grilled livers and other innards along with the poached eggs; with that you don't need bacon too much. (No coffee . . .) Sitting between Claudius and Ethan—hovering, rather, too excited to eat sensibly herself, needing to touch the men every now and then to be sure they were real, or make a seeming-casual trip to the window—Eve presently asked, "Claudius, about the rifle— I suppose it was the tiger made you want to carry one, and where did you—oh, God love a duck, I haven't even given Ethan a chance to tell about the horse! Look, I have a problem: how are you going to tell and explain both at once when I won't permit it? And, Mama, were you like this? I mean, always in perfect command of yourself and knowing exactly what you were doing but never having a grain of sense?"

"Yes," said Alma Newman. "I thought just then I heard—"

"Yes," said Eve softly and jumped up white around the lips and ran out of the house.

In the small following quiet Claudius studied the new Ethan Nye, this thoughtful, almost cautious-appearing man. Would Bellamy be as greatly changed? He said, "Long summer, Eth? Go north the way you planned?"

"Yes. A lake, and mountains . . ." Ethan's face suggested he had more to say, questions, perhaps; but there was now a murmuring of voices beyond the door, and that would be troubling him. "I never knew," Ethan said. "I can't just describe—"

"High and closely massed, white granite faces."

"You know them, then."

"A little. I was born the other side of them."

"I knew them," said Alma Newman. "I used to know

them, and the sound of waterfalls. The brooks swollen to anger in the spring, and the hemlocks, the sudden storms . . . We create our own ends, our own purposes, don't we? Within the limits nature sets. My purpose, if I had my way, would be to see the White Mountains again. And since that is outside the limits nature has set for me, still I see them, in here, in my fashion, I do see them, the white granite and the early sun."

"We should have known more clearly in the old time that men create their own purposes," said Claudius. "We could always dither over the question, What's the end of existence?, never noticing that if you can grow a good crop of wheat, or carve a good apple-wood billikin, or write a symphony, then the wheat or the billikin or the symphony *is* one of the ends of existence. Maybe the hankering after meaningful achievement was one reason why we bred so furiously in the last decades: begetting a child is so obviously an achievement that can't be cried down, even if we know all we've done is transmit the genes, and remember that old coelacanth did as much."

"Coelacanth?" said Ethan. But Ethan was a divided man, his question asked with only a part of his attention. Claudius in his own uncertainty could sympathize. The red-bearded boy might as well have groaned aloud, "Why in *hell* can't they come in the house?"

"Coelacanth was an ancient type of queer fish," said Claudius, "that survived into modern times. It was important to the study of vertebrate development, and also demonstrates how some clumsy constructions go blundering on from age to age—like marriage, trousers, theology—blundering on because they more or less work, or because they haven't yet come up against anything capable of sweeping them away. I remember . . ." Then he and Ethan were on their feet, relieved from the tension of half listening, making acceptable noises of greeting to the dark and friendly young man who seemed to both of them pretty much a stranger.

Bellamy had entered the kitchen without his glasses— Eve's arm was around him and she had, perhaps, been crying a little—but he put them on before he shook hands. He said, "I expected to find you discussing almost anything on earth except the coelacanth." He pronounced *coelacanth* (the *Notes* say) without a tremor, but was of course not asked to spell the brute.

"Well, we're peculiar in other ways," said Claudius. "For instance, I ate up all the chicken giblets."

"You just thought you did," said Eve, and her frying pan hissed in confirmation.

Kenneth Bellamy watched her hands and lips overcome their unsteadiness. He could feel her undiminished need of him; and yet what might have been certainty in himself or in both of them last May was no such thing now. Why, that flush remaining in her face might come simply from the heat of the old stove chewing up soft maple. (More would have to be cut.)

After she set a plate in front of Bellamy and poured him a glass of water from a Wedgwood pitcher that had been her great-grandmother's and started more eggs to poaching, it was Ethan she leaned against, that sweet soft hip against his shoulder; it was Claudius she smiled for; it was Ethan whose hair she caught in fierce tender fingers to tilt his face back and gaze down at him. "Oh, you are all so . . . so . . ."

"What's the girl up to at the moment?" Alma Newman asked. "I swear, Eve, I don't know where you ever got your emotional nature. Your father was a quiet man, and you certainly never saw me give way to my feelings."

"Oh, never! Why, Mama, you're the wildest weirdie of the lot of us, and you know it. You're not fooling the Bear-Strangler or anyone else." And she said gently, "Caleb, sit down over there by the door where you always do. Breakfast soon. You don't mind having him here, do you? He doesn't drool."

"Sit down, Caleb," said Bellamy. "Sit down, old man."

"He's only a part of the human condition," said Claudius. "A reminder, in a way. A sort of suppose-the-genes-went-thataway."

"You're still kind of tough to understand," said Ethan Nye. "I spent some part of this summer thinking about different things you've said."

"I was born fifty-one years ago in the state of Maine. Don't take me too seriously. Well, Ken, in a few words, where you been?"

"Reading," said Bellamy, and he could feel in his shirt pocket the curious weight of the diamonds. Eve had probably noticed the angular hardness when he kissed her. He had said then, "It's a trifling present for you, if you want it when you've heard the story of it. Tell you later."

She had exclaimed, "No, no! Everything about love and life and all that in the next thirty seconds." And then the long-desired pressure of her mouth that ruled out speech.

After the kiss he had been the first to lower his gaze and scrape his moccasin along the flagstones; and then came Caleb gibbering and romping and wagging his hind end like a dog, requiring the blessing of human speech before he would quiet down—the poor monster might have been hugging his leg in another moment if Eve hadn't spoken a little sharply and told him to go sit down somewhere. Then she too was standing with downcast eyes and pushing her foot across the stones, and she said, "The others are here. Claudius looks well. Ethan found himself a beautiful horse."

"He—uh—did?"

"Uh. In the barn."

"Found it in a—"

"Stupid. Found it somewhere. Now in the—ai-yi-yi-yi." Then they had been laughing (Caleb gobbling in the background) and each needing the assurance of the other's peace of mind that laughter might or might not bring. "Ah, Ken, how do *I* know? The answer to the question you haven't asked, and no asking it right now, I forbid it. Come in and have your breakfast, and I promised you that nature will—will take its course. Isn't that what nature does? I *know* I've read somewhere that it does."

According to this our version of the legend of the Judgment of Eve, which *ought* to please you well enough so that you can chuck all the others or at least let the kids have them to cut up into funny shapes for a Project in Social Studies, that was the sum of the private conversation outside the kitchen door which put such a strain on Claudius Gardiner and Ethan Nye and Alma Newman that by the time it broke up they were fairly advanced squirrel meat.

"Just reading," said Bellamy. "Oh, I ran down to Hartford a couple-three days. Library was okay but no better. Nice trip. Of course a lot of the reading was still over my head. Gaps. Questions that would go buzzing through me too fast to jot down a note. Problems I could have been tackling in childhood if . . . For instance, Claudius, why did the existentialists have to drown themselves in such a pea-green sea of unnecessary verbiage? Seemed like such a promising start, and then flufflephooph."

"I think they missed out some on freshman biology," said Claudius. "It could have given them perspective." And the little man went on as Bellamy had hoped he would, with some help from Mrs. Newman, so that Bellamy could finish the noble breakfast at leisure and study the wonderful stranger girl across the table from him, and the challenging gravity, the new thoughtfulness of Ethan Nye.

2. The Judgment

After breakfast Eve declared the law for the remainder of the day. "We shall loaf around," she said, "and be happy for a while. I'd like to show you the barn, the fields where Caleb has worked so hard, some of the woods if you like, and the typewriter my father used, maybe my Great-Grandmother Anderson's Paisley shawls if Mama thinks it would be all right to take them out. And we'll talk, and you shall tell me what's been happening this long time, and perhaps we could have some make-believe stories too—because I remember a lot of those and others have sometimes happened like rockets inside my own head— this head, imagine?—and the one and only form of talk that's forbidden is to ask me any questions about me, until after supper. Then we'll break out the last of my father's wine, and I promise to tell you—as well as I can—how it is with me, after you have—maybe—told me what is love. But first a day to enjoy our reunion, a day of *small* pleasures—and you know what? Mama tells me they did have those even in the twentieth century, in spite of being so damned grim and progressive and vinegar-puss about everything in their mis'ble old books."

From that lawmaking of Eve's for the day derives a whole amazing collection of literary oddments—*Tales of East Redfield, An Afternoon with Eve, The Hundred and One Stories, The Literary Background of Ancient Massachusetts, Eve's Anecdotes—Fable or Commitment?*—wah, wah, wah—which add up to enough words per minute to have kept Scheherazade's neck in splendid flexible condition for at least nine months. One of these mishmash jobs (title herewith suppressed) includes a triple-jointed think-piece absurdly attributed to Claudius Gardiner: *Novelist as Shadow-Boxer: Being a Short Final Analysis of Late-Twentieth-Century Trends.* Now, it's been admitted that Gardiner wasn't perfect, but this thing Pure twenty-fifth-century literary criticism at its inveterate worst. Homer had them too, you know, same as Homer's old pup had fleas.

Be assured, nothing of that golden and lightly windy October day shall be included here except the three (imperfect) narratives that were offered to Eve, and their amendments, until that lovely woman (oh, sorry, girls: for the day she was wearing a brown skirt down to about here, leaf-brown, you might call it, with an emerald-green short-sleeved blouse, and natural-leather moccasins of a kind you obviously can't get because she made them herself) that lovely woman found herself too busy (no stockings) getting supper to listen to any more talk. She heard:

"It was like discovering morning for the first time, or never having seen the grass. I'd been living behind a veil of half-vision without guessing the extent of my deprivation. Eve, I wish I could tell you everything about that cobweb in the sun—the sunlight itself so mild because it came through a grimy window, but it could show me the wing of a fly in the web, and turn that into a diamond. Your eyes are good—they must be or they wouldn't be looking through me the way they do—and so you've always been able to see such marvels and take them for granted. . . . After that, Claudius and I parted company. Do you know, Claudius, I watched you march down that avenue and out of sight without really thinking of the moving figure as you at all, I was that full of astonishment at my own sight, too full of the discovery to wonder about you or wonder where you meant to go. I do recall another sort of wondering, though. I wondered how many others may be living in a similar blindness, how many may have done so in the past, even less aware of it than I was. . . . After we separated, I started to leave the city by a road to the west. I was thinking of all those abandoned places, the dwellings, even more the shops, all the different kinds and none to take care of them or trade there any more. I . . . looked into some of them, on my way to a bridge that crosses a big river on the western side of the city.

And in one I found . . . these, Eve. A couple of old skeletons were lying on the floor. May have been some pitiful fight to the death long ago, over these or things like them, perhaps. They were in a strongbox sort of thing, and the door of it was open—rusted open, in fact. From what I've learned in the books I think they must be diamonds. I'd like you to have them, unless the thought of that long-ago fighting would spoil them for you. . . . Well, then I did cross the bridge and start west, and I'd gone about half a morning's walk—morning, no, it was afternoon, wasn't it? —when I ran into something I didn't know existed in this world. I got information about that too from the books, later on. An enormous cat-creature, pale-tawny, stripes of a darker shade, like the pictures of tigers I suppose you've seen. He was coming down the road toward me as if he owned it—well, he did. I climbed a tree, but then when I saw he was going on toward Redfield I made myself get down and follow. I can't exactly explain it. Maybe my new glasses made me reckless. It's true I was thinking of you, Claudius, but I can't honestly claim a definite purpose of going along your road to warn you. Still I did follow him —at a pretty safe distance and keeping near the trees, I assure you—back as far as the city. Maybe I wasn't too keen on going west, either. By the bridge he went down to drink from the river, and—I think I was a little out of my mind—I shot an arrow at him. Looking down at him from the bridge, I guess that made me feel big. Got him in the foreleg. Luckily for me, he panicked and ran.

"Ran south, Claudius, and my silly courage or whatever it was sort of gave out then. I knew I couldn't catch up with him, and you were long gone. I didn't know if you meant to keep on along the main road. Maybe that kind of courage carries only just so far, and then we have to back off and admit our failures. Fact remains I should've tried to catch up with you and I didn't.

"I didn't go west again either. Stayed there in Redfield —well, that one trip I mentioned, but that was much later in the summer—and made a home for myself in the public library. Oh, the poor scrubby bundle of books in Shelter Town! I'd never begun to guess. Why, Eve, I've been a dozen times around the planet, which is round and large, an uncommon garden. Well, with your books here, you know such pleasures, but I never did before. The great stories—I've read Homer, Sophocles, Virgil. Shakespeare, of course—oh, but so many I haven't come to yet! I'll go back there—with you, I hope. The history—maybe the history was better than all but the greatest of the stories. The sciences—I've only nibbled there. At random. I need a guide, anyone does, in that. . . . A cut diamond is a prism that takes the sun's light, and by its own nature, its imperfections, breaks up the light into a thousand colors and fires to make human eyes a little wiser, a little happier. Love is a diamond that takes the light of life and gives it back to us tranfigured. Will you wear these now and then because I love you?"

And later in the day, unhappy in her mind, Eve heard:

"The Manchurian tiger, the one I spoke of in the note I left for you, must have been the same one. He was limping a little in the left foreleg when I saw him. In the old days there'd have been a few pairs existing in American zoos. I saw some in Chicago, I think in 1968. They're considerably bigger than Bengal tigers, and light-colored as Ken described it. And I remember some newspaper story back before the one-day war, about some lunatic who managed to free some of the wild things from the zoos in several cities. He liberated only the dangerous ones, the story had it, some poor paranoid with a grudge fight against the human race. Well, that limping tiger I saw was a young beast; it would have to be a descendant of a zoo escape.

"After I saw him, on my way south, I came back to Redfield, where I'd noticed a sporting-goods store with a few unopened cases of rifles. Hadn't wanted them then. Remarkable how fast you can change your mind. I got this one, and with it I followed his trail for a day, came up with him in the early evening—and I missed. All the same he's vulnerable flesh and blood; he and his like can be met by men who face them with the right weapons and the right skill at the right time.

"I came back this way, Eve, and left that note on your porch to warn you, and then I went on to carry the same warning to those other people I told you of, who may join us here, or somewhere. I told them I would come and see them again before long. Some had died, one or two children have been born.

"I brought you back only myself a little older. I know that what seems to be love often is not, or it is but ceases to be maybe in no more time than it takes a sigh of delight to spend itself. I know there are many kinds of love, as there are many kinds of truth, and one kind of love is a complexity which can occasionally grow—rather slowly, I'd say—between people who respect as well as love each other, and this kind of love can last as long as time and chance will allow any individual's happiness to last. It can make the fortunate lifetime productive and sweet, and the unfortunate one at worst endurable."

And she heard:

"I've told you already about the lake and how I stayed there, maybe too long. There's a magic in that place, but dreaming a long time, I guess it's not my way, and one thing that pulled me out of that dead end was a glimpse of blue-white triangle against the sky, a hint of mountains. Somehow I knew what it was, though there was nothing like that near Shelter Town. And some thought—it could have been partly old fairy tales—made me wonder if gods could live in such hills as that. Ai-yah, they didn't show themselves to me, but I had the thought and so might as well speak of it. I came to an old-time road that led to the summit of one of the mountains, and it was up in that country I found my horse.

"He belonged to a man who—well, I had to fight with him. I think he was mad. Governor Talbot, he called himself, and someway he'd made himself ruler of a little village. Lord, there were only seven families but he had to be king of it. I ran into him and a couple of his people on the road, he made trouble for me and then he was about to kill one of his men who defended me—so what happened was we fought, and he died, Eve. But he died awful easy, somehow, as if it might have been his heart giving out instead of any licks I gave him. Sort of a big bogeyman that turns into nothing at all if you face him.

"They were good people in that village. You'll want to see them, Claudius, but chances are they wouldn't move from that place. They're so full of hard-luck talk about the stony ground they'd never be happy any place where they couldn't be cussing it. I couldn't tell if they held Governor Talbot's death against me or if they were glad to be shut of him, or both. I don't like having his death on my hands, but still, he would have killed that other man. I keep thinking the villagers could have got rid of him themselves if they'd really been a-mind to. It's a puzzle.

"I saw your tiger up there, or one like him, on a ridge

maybe half a mile from me. I watched for any trail of him on the way back, but didn't find it.

"That barn out there needs a lot of repair, Eve, and those pines, they really ought to be pushed back before they swallow up too much of the good land. I'd admire to see a fence around the property too, keep the sheep in, permanent pasture for horses—not that Caleb hasn't done a good job with the spring spading and so on—I can see that—but you need a man on the place, and there ought to be more than just a garden patch.

"I'd do . . . things like that, and there'd be our sons to do it after our time. Maybe that's all I can tell you in words about what love is."

After which Eve was much too busy cooking supper to listen—that is, according to this version, and never mind the gaudy one with the language cribbed out of Malory, which has Caleb preparing the baked meats after being sent back ywis to the scullery, as if he could've managed it, as if Eve would have allowed him in the scullery if she'd had one, whatever a scullery is. Ethan Nye was enlisted to bring chairs again, and spread a tablecloth, and tend the fires in the kitchen stove and the living room. Kenneth Bellamy set out glasses and silverware, carried up the wine from the cellar, and did other miscellaneous fetching and carrying with Caleb getting underfoot. Alma Newman and Claudius Gardiner talked again of old times and other places, with some discussion of Dr. Stuyvesant and structural phonology, and of how her childhood had been shadowed by the Second World War and his by the 1960s.

They continued that discourse a little, after Eve called them to supper. "Every generation," Alma Newman was saying, "must have heard thunder on the left. Ours happened to get more of a direct hit, that was all. So long as we continue I suppose we're still Earth's best candidates for interstellar journeying some day, if we can just worry through another thousand years or so."

"I understand from my reading," said Kenneth Bellamy, "that in 1970 they were thinking seriously of an interstellar expedition, and not as anything glorious but just as a kind of hurry-up, last-minute effort to save something from this planet before we ruined it. It was to have been some kind of vehicle capable of journeying indefinitely while the passengers had children and grew old and

died and were reassimilated, until the thing reached some
other part of the galaxy, to colonize. There was a little
bunch of crackpots—science-fiction writers, I think they
were called, for some undecipherable reason—who'd been
discussing the idea for years, until it was ready to be advanced in 1970 as a revolutionary new proposal and quite
serious. Do you remember that talk, Claudius?"

"Oh, sure. Carefully selected passengers. It would have
been tried, with a little more time. For that matter, it's possible it *was* tried. Pretty hard to keep anything like that
under wraps; still, the public had grown more and more
apathetic year by year, more and more willing to let Big
Brother decide what it should know."

Eve asked, "Who was going to select the passengers?"

"Why, in the '70s most citizens would have meekly as-
sumed that only the politicos were in a position to do it.
And so the politicos would have done it, with probably a
committee of tame professors and safe celebrities approving, and a subcommittee of fairly wild professors off on
the left proclaiming the whole thing was a bust. Several
criteria would have been agreed on by all—for example,
all passengers would have had to be wholesome but not
fanatic Christians, plus a few Jews. No atheists or agnostics
need apply. On paper, the racial groups would have been
figured out in decent percentages, I suppose. But then in
practice, when the balloon was actually ready to go up,
I'm afraid at least ninety per cent of the passengers would
have been somebody's relatives, including Cousin Henry
who wasn't quite bright."

"You're still bitter about the old time, aren't you?"

"Well, Eve, I lived in it. I loved it too. Somewhere between love and bitterness I try to find the truth about it."

"What is truth?" said Alma Newman. "No, at this dinner table maybe we don't need the cold wind of the great
questions. Still in my old age I seem to have lost a lot of
my patience with lies. Telling lies to avoid giving pain for
instance—it's not good, merely a choice of the lesser evil,
if the pain is thought to be the greater one. You grow up
threading your way through those and the other gray al-
ternatives. You grow up and learn how purpose, and good
and evil, and justice, are all human creations, necessary
and I'd say noble, and thoroughly human. You grow up,
finding how many other human constructions are anything
but noble, such as the notion of the ethical absolute. But

as for truth, why, I was brought up to believe that to know the truth as far as you can is good, and to speak it is nearly always more good than evil. I still believe it and I expect to die believing it."

"Eve," said Kenneth Bellamy, "may I fill your glass? This is what happened. On my way to that bridge I met a woman who was a little mad from living a quarter-century alone. She must have been somewhere in the forties, beautiful too in a wild, artificial sort of way. She took me to the place where she was living. I was snared by a feeling that I think is not to be trusted—pity. And partly by lust and partly by a damn feeble inability to say no when it it may have been what I wanted to say. She had collected things from here and there in the ruined city—foraging, she called it. She was managing to believe the old world still existed somehow and functioned around her. I helped her with the make-believe. I don't think I regret that too much. I do regret committing myself to the identity she gave me—she was trying to believe I was her husband who died or went away twenty-five years ago—when I knew I couldn't stay with her. The necklace is one of many pieces of jewelry she'd foraged for herself. I spent one night with her and sneaked away before she waked, with the necklace, a common thief. What I told you about meeting the tiger on the road was true, but it was the thought of Grace, not of Claudius, that made me trail the brute back to the city and try to shoot him. It's curious. I could play along with her madness and steal from her and walk out on her, but I couldn't bear to think of the tiger snatching her up like a cat grabbing a sparrow. So I did go back and shot him, and he ran. Then I went to the place where she lived, and I found her dead. She'd drunk almost a full quart of whisky. That could kill, couldn't it, Claudius?"

"Yes."

"The rest was true as I told it, Eve. I was . . . still pitying her. I even dug a grave. Isn't a grave an almost perfect demonstration of the emptiness of that kind of pity? Perhaps there are useful kinds—I can't quite think that out. I knew while I dug the grave that I was only trying to appease myself, to hide from the fact that I was glad and relieved that she had died and solved my problems for me. Well, I settled down in the public library and tried to let some light into my head."

Eve let her hand remain covering his on the tablecloth

a moment, and then cleared away the emptied plates, and presently she was saying, "Bear-Strangler, what are you doing over there by the window? The moonlight can't be any prettier than I am, and if you stay over there you'll miss out on some important drinking and the sharing of peculiar thoughts."

"Hoo boy," he said, "can't have that." He came back, and she filled his glass, and he asked, "Mrs. Newman, would you say we owe other people the whole truth about ourselves?"

"We do not. We owe it to ourselves, as much as we can take of it anyhow. I suppose we owe others any part of it that directly affects their lives and that we think them able to understand—but, dear Ethan, it gets complicated there. If you tell your heart's business to a fool he can only make a fool's work of it, and no purpose served."

"But if you love someone, you owe a great deal of truth?"

"I think you do, Ethan. Lies justified by the flavor of romantic love—that's sanctified eyewash. To love only your own fanciful image of a person is an insult to the person's actual self, a way of saying that what he is doesn't matter, all that matters is your uninformed notion of what you'd like him to be, or what you think he ought to be, might be. In other words, boy, if you love my daughter you'll have to give her credit for at least half as much brains as her mother has."

"Well, Eve, the story I told you—I think it's all straight enough, except that I'll never know whether I wrestled that man mostly because he was trying to kill a weaker one or because I had to show my beef was better than his. He was—some-way he was *like* me, Eve, like me gone sour and crazy. He was every dirty and foolish thing I could be if I ever started using all this strength against my own people instead of for them. And then—well, I've called myself simple, made sort of a habit of it. But I remember you saw through that, back last May. Now I can see too, when I say that it's a sham. I'm not simple, I'm just ignorant. I'm as complicated as any of you, but I've been too lazy or scared or ignorant to look inside. I guess I need the books too. And I'll read them. I love you, Eve. I won't plow away all my brains into the furrow."

"Claudius, I don't think you need to make any corrections."

"Ah, Nora, no, no, I don't think so. Except to say again that I was born in another world and I'm growing old."

"My dear, do you know you called me Nora?"

"I did, didn't I? And still it's in this present world that I love you. Human beings have always had to find out about living in more than one world. To fall asleep in a world of shivering and wake up into courage. To wake out of indifference into love. To wake out of childhood into . . . something else."

Eve stood in the candlelight with her glass of golden wine and said, "As a last small pleasure before I tell you my decision—and I will, I will, that is if all of you still love me—let's drink to every kind of waking!"

All of those who told the legend in the past and sometimes wrote it down were agreed in saying the ending of it was happy, even for Caleb, who died young (trying to strangle a bear, according to one or two miserably edited versions). And they say that Alma Newman lived on for several years and died comfortably in her sleep—that's good; that we accept. And they say that after Eve announced her judgment there was no heart-burning or jealousy—oh, that's good also, and may even be true, though not everyone would necessarily swear to it on the Unabridged.

As the banquet ended, the old lady told some story out of the past, not quite remembering she had told it before —it may have been the one about the stalled bus. And there began a marriage which endured with as much happiness as can be expected when the contestants are well matched and the qualities of laughter and kindness never too long forgotten. Forever afterward is considerably too long for human patience; besides, it brings up the touchy question of human mortality. But this marriage did endure until Eve herself, lovely Eve with the blue-green eyes, grew old and died, and in her old age there were grownup grandchildren who were tactful enough to let her tell the story of her judgment as often as she pleased—the great-grandchildren also listened to it peacefully on rainy days —and she never told it twice in exactly the same words.

As for the ending of it, finding your own answer is simply what Claudius would have called a necessary part of the human condition.

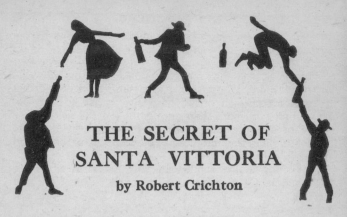

THE SECRET OF
SANTA VITTORIA

by Robert Crichton

THE NATION'S #1 BESTSELLER

From time immemorial the Italian hill town of Santa Vittoria had existed as a world unto itself, hostile to strangers, wholly involved in growing and making the fat black wine that was its glory and its lifeblood. As the Allied armies approached, the Germans sent an occupying force to claim the town's great treasure—one million bottles of wine. At this moment a leader emerged—the clownish wine merchant Bombolini. Behind him the town united, forgetting ancient feuds, lovers' rivalries, the division between aristocrat and peasant, pooling its energies and resources to outwit the invader.

"This brilliant novel should be celebrated with a fanfare of trumpets, with festivals in the streets." —*The New York Times*

"Crichton tells his story with grace, pace, warmth, and a wonderful free-reeling wit that skips among the vineyards like an inebriated billygoat." —*Time Magazine*

95¢

If you cannot obtain copies of this title at your local bookseller's, just send the price (plus 10c per copy for handling and postage) to Dell Books, Box 2291, Grand Central Post Office, New York, N Y 10017. No postage or handling charge is required on any order of five or more books